THE MARKETER

ANOTHER BERLIN STORY

ANTONIO LA MATINA

ragingsloths

Part I

If you want to know who is the smartest person in any organization forget about the executives. Instead ask for the interns for they have the brightest and least corrupted minds. Even though university studies partially spoiled their original creativity, their spirit is almost intact compared with other members of the team. They are prepared to cope with uncertainty and therefore their minds are more flexible and ready to do whatever it takes to reach their objective. The higher you climb the hierarchy, the less smart or interesting people you will meet until you get to the CEO, by far the most half-witted mind of them all. He is envious of the creativity the interns possess and therefore he keeps giving them humiliating tasks to make sure that soon they become empty human shells - just like him.

I'm rambling now. Well, let's cut the shit and try to make some sense of this thing. To be fair to you, if sense is what you hope to find here, you might as well end this reading now and go check your newsfeed. Though you will find very little of it there too. Don't say I didn't warn you.

It was the day after Steve Jobs died, but this is a different story from a different place.

The open-plan must have been 150 square meters at best, with endless rows of desks adorned by screens, keyboards, Starbucks tumblers, telephones, and cables that spurted like the black arteries of some perverse cybernetic organism; a Moloch that fed on the lymph of the people attached to it. A swarm of people peering lifelessly into their computer screens, not showing the slightest sign of interest in me being there in that particular moment.

I was standing in the hallway, contemplating all that human misery when a long bony hand got hold of my shoulder.

"Welcome, Tony. Shall we begin your onboarding?" Eva Rauschenberg, the Head of Human Resources, said with a stilted British accent. She was the only person I had seen in that place wearing formal clothes.

She guided me through that maze of cables, desks, and flesh to the CEOs' office and knocked on the glass door.

A large man opened it. "You must be the new Italian intern," he grinned. "Welcome to Go-Go Fashion. I am Kaspar Ulli, the arm of this company, and this is Benjamin Riedle, he is the brain." Kaspar pointed at his partner, who in return said nothing. Benjamin stared at me for a few seconds, with those dull eyes, baring his huge incisors. His thinning red hair stressed his sickly appearance.

Benjamin nodded before returning to his business.

We left the CEOs and Eva invited me to attend a presentation about the story of Go-Go Fashion. As we entered the meeting room, four people were already sitting on the benches facing the white screen. Eva asked each of us to introduce ourselves to the rest.

"I'm Ekaterina, from Ukraine."

"My name is Alex and I come from Nürnberg."

"Leandro from Brazil."

"Hi everyone, I'm Rocio, from Spain."

I was last. "I'm Tony and I come from Italy."

Eva began the presentation. The first slides recounted how Kaspar and Benjamin had the idea to create an online fashion store and founded the company in Kaspar's backroom, three years earlier. Every tech company's story that aspires to be taken seriously needs to have some garage, basement, storage room or backroom at some point in its narration. Even better if one of the founders drops out of university to pursue his startup dream. May God or Steve Jobs's ghost strike me dead if I ever decide to found a company sitting my ass cozily on the couch of my living room.

Kaspar grew up with a passion for luxury garments, thanks to his mother who ran a sewing lab in the district of Mitte, while Benjamin was born a geek. The biographical slides showed respectively a picture of a chubby young Kaspar – he must have been about twelve – wearing a suit and a fedora which somehow reminded me of a very little version of Joe Pesci in *Goodfellas*, and of a seventeen-year-old Benjamin as he happily sat in front of a computer giving the thumbs-up sign to the photographer.

It went on explaining how the two young entrepreneurs obtained their first investment round and how, later, they received financial backup from the notorious venture builder Platypusnetic.

"Do you have questions?" Eva asked. She had a stern look and kept her arms folded as she spoke.

No one raised their hand.

After the presentation, it was Lucia's turn to continue my onboarding. She was my team leader, the one in charge of the Italian market.

We sat at a long dining table in the cafeteria and she showed me through the website. It had countless shopping categories. Shoes, clothing, accessories, beauty products, and so on. Then there were the subcategories: high heels, sneakers, t-shirts, short-sleeved t-shirts, long-sleeved t-shirts, low sneakers, high sneakers, jumpers, sweaters, ponchos, summer jackets, winter jackets, shirts with Kent collar, shirts with shark collar, and on and on. For each of those, they required the interns like me to write a text of 500 words.

"You must repeat the keyword at least three times in each text," she said.

"You mean the name of the product?" I asked.

"If you're writing an article about high-neck pullovers, then the keywords are *high-neck pullover*."

"Wouldn't it make the text look unnatural?"

"Perhaps… I don't know. It is for you to make it nice," she studied me behind the humongous glass frames that covered half of her gaunt face, revealing the dark purplish eyebags that fell on her cheekbones.

"Got it," I said.

Every day we had to write at least eight original copies based on a list of products that someone or a bot generated and sent to us via email.

Dear Jedi,
We need your superpowers to write the following texts
and help us defeat the Phantom Menace.
We trust you will not disappoint us!

Whether I was a Jedi, a ninja, or neither of the two, the job seemed easy, even for those 400 euros a month.

I was sitting at my desk, working on my first article when Eva approached Lucia who at that moment was intent at peeling a pear. For some reason, the skin of the pear resting on the surface of her desk, without using a napkin or a plate, irritated me. The others didn't seem to mind.

I heard Eva whisper something to Lucia, then Lucia pointed her finger, smeared with the juice of the pear, at me and another intern sitting next to me. Eva then leaned toward the two of us, gave a condescending smile and asked us to follow her to the cafeteria.

In the cafeteria a pile of IKEA boxes containing desks and office chairs lay on the floor.

"Do you know how to assemble them?" Eva asked me.

"Sure," I said and she walked off.

Massimo, the other intern, had already begun ripping the first box with a cutter. He showed no hesitation.

"Do you do this often?" I asked him as I knelt on the floor, working the screws inside the pre-drilled holes of the desks.

"Last week I did it twice, the one before three times. They ask the interns to do this for the newcomers and the seniors," he said with a sharp and dignified look.

"They didn't mention it in the contract," I said jokingly.

"They ask us to do other things, you will see, like loading and unloading the dishwasher after lunch break, or going grocery shopping for the office stocks," he said.

We each had a desk and a chair to assemble. People walked by, not paying attention to us. They talked to each other, looked at their phones and sipped their filtered coffee.

"It's better than serving pizzas for five euros an hour," Massimo said while mending a table leg. "Besides, if we play our cards well, perhaps in one or two years we will be managers ourselves and will tell other underpaid clueless interns to write the fucking articles," he grinned. "A friend of mine is working on a farm in Australia, he moved there six months ago. His main responsibility is to keep the birds away from the harvest."

"Do they dress him like a scarecrow?"

"I don't think so. He just chases them off."

"How?"

"When he sees one coming, he dashes from one side of the crop field to the other screaming like a madman and wielding a stick."

We finished assembling the desks and returned to our seats. I wrote four product descriptions that afternoon. The products ranged from designer handbags and mid-season ankle boots to sneakers. Despite the dreariness of the topics, the words flew. I finished the first three articles in one hour, until I got stuck with leg warmers.

"How could one come up with five hundred words about leg warmers?" I asked Massimo.

He showed me a few texts written by other people. "Do you notice anything?" he said.

"Sure, they are incredibly dull," I said.

"Don't you see all these articles are carbon copies?"

They all presented the same structure. A catchy introduction of the product accompanied by fashionable words such as *trendy, inspiring, fresh, must-have, iconic, statement*, and *smart,* followed by pop culture references of famous people wearing such clothes or accessories in movies, TV shows, or commercials, and the job was done. And the keywords repeated in every paragraph.

"Are there people who read this crap?" I asked.

"Of course not. These are SEO-texts."

"Lucia mumbled something about SEO during the training."

"It stands for Search Engine Optimization. You stuff a text with specific keywords, in this case *leg warmers*, and your website page will be shown to the people that search for it on Google."

Lucia left at 6 pm sharp, the rest of the team followed shortly after. So did I.

When I got home Marina had just taken a shower. I liked the smell of the coconut milk on her wet brown hair. It felt like home. Life made sense again at home. She was building a joint on the kitchen table.

"How was it?" She jumped from the chair all excited.

"I had to assemble a desk and a chair," I said. I was relieved to be home, didn't feel much like talking about my first day at work. "How was your day?" I asked her.

"Did they ask you to assemble a desk and a chair on your first day?" Her excitement had blown over a bit.

"This guy I met told me he does it almost every day. Apparently it's a common thing to ask interns to do."

"What about the job?" She was now fixing the joint with her saliva.

"I have to write texts about shoes, bags, and shit that no one will ever read, so this desks business is not a bad thing after all."

"What do they make you write them for?"

"SEO, it has something to do with Google. Go figure."

"I'm glad to see you have already got the hang of it," she said mockingly. "Got a light?"

I handed her my lighter, she took one puff from the joint and passed it to me.

"What about Jabba, how is that old sleaze doing?" Jabba was Marina's boss at her catering job and, in case you wondered, that was not his actual name.

"You didn't even know who Jabba the Hutt was before meeting me."

"And I thank you for that, you sexy nerdy freak," I said. "You know I'm more of an *Alien*-kind-of-guy. God bless Ellen Ripley."

"He proposed to Suzanna," she said.

"Jabba proposed to your colleague?" I began coughing.

"Yes."

"No shit," I tried to clear my throat.

"They are flying to Las Vegas next month."

"That's our Jabba. Will he finally stop hitting on you and the others then?"

The catering agency Marina worked for organized events for corporations, like banks and insurance companies. Most of the guys and girls who worked there were students that needed to pay their university fees. She wanted to become a high-school teacher of Italian. She had a plan; at least one of us did.

"They sent home a girl today," Marina said, while I took another puff.

"Did she call Jabba a fat sleaze?"

"She was responsible for the cloakroom and was approached by some Cruella de Vil type who demanded her to go fetch her mink fur."

"It's early October," I said. "Who wears a fur in October? What's a mink, anyway? Don't think I have ever seen one."

"We wondered the same. Anyhow, when my colleague told her that she couldn't find the fur, the woman went mad and began screaming at her things like 'that fur costs more than what you will earn in your lifetime. I want my fur now or there will be blood.'"

"What did the girl do?"

"She broke into tears. We thought she was having a panic attack. Then Jabba showed up and sent her home."

"What about the fur?"

"It turned out the fur was not in the cloakroom. Cruella gave it to her assistant who left it in the car thinking it was safer."

We took a few more hits of the joint while preparing dinner and ate, then sat on the couch in the living room, finished the joint and watched a movie on the computer. *Wings of Desire*, I think that was.

We had been living in that apartment in Sonnenallee since my arrival in the city, two weeks earlier. The guy who sublet to us was traveling in Brazil for six months. The Germans and their *Wanderlust*. It was an *Altbau* of about fifty square meters. High ceilings with posters and flags of Saint Pauli Football Club hanging from the walls and ethnic objects meticulously distributed in the apartment.

We went to bed. The whole Sonnenallee, with its kebab kiosks and *Spätkaufs* went silent. The only noise I could hear was the neighbor getting back home and working the key inside the door lock. I tried to imagine the next day at work.

Marina leaned on my chest. Her long hair tickled my nostrils, her eyes were closed, and that dimple that crossed her chin looked even more gorgeous under the feeble night lights that made their way through the curtains.

How good it is to be home.

It was a dark and silent place. My feet felt a clammy surface as I was standing barefoot. It was cold yet I felt a strange warmth rising from my guts. As I struggled to walk on that swampy mass, my paces made a soggy noise. I walked through a bunch of hedges toward what looked like a group of ancient gravestones forming a circle that delimited a small hill.

At the top of the hill, I saw a young woman. She was on her knees and wore a light tunic that revealed her pale skin under the moonlight and she had long, fair hair. She had a catatonic look, and I thought she was beautiful for some reason.

Her arms were spread, and hanging from one of them I saw those filthy claws. Obscenely long nails that spurted out of grey, bony hands. They belonged to something that squatted beside her. At first I couldn't discern it from the shadows. It looked like a very old woman or what was left of her.

Her grip on the girl's left arm was firm as she was grinding the flesh with the few teeth attached to that hole that didn't look like a human mouth anymore, but rather that of a giant worm due to its festering circular shape. Her eyes were lifeless anemic balls and her skull was only in part covered by a black mass of slick hair.

That creature relentlessly kept tearing tissue apart from the arm of the girl, her eyes wide open in triumphant fury and blood dripped from her decaying jaw. The noise of the torn flesh cracked throughout the field, painful like needles shot into my ears, one after the other.

The young woman was still and comatose, but I glimpsed a hint of ecstasy on her face, and I could hear the feeble noises she was making that sounded like soft groans.

Something prevented me from trying to help that girl or even to run away. I just stood there watching.

Then the creature gave a sign of having seen me. She stared at me with those lifeless, ghastly bulbs as she kept munching on the girl's arm. I must have been less than ten meters away. She grinned at me. I could see inside that bloody cavity of sharp teeth and flesh. She kept grinning, chewing and staring at me for an inconceivable amount of time.

Then I heard something behind me. It was almost imperceptible, like the noise of grass that bends under the weight of something creeping on it. I turned around, and I saw half a dozen more of those hideous creatures dragging themselves toward me with those repulsive grins and ghastly eyeballs.

I woke up and looked at my phone. 4 am. I like to wake up in the middle of the night knowing that there is still time to sleep.

The alarm rang at 8 am. Marina didn't hear it. I showered and skipped breakfast to rush to the U-Bahn station.

On my second day of work, Eva asked me to assemble another desk, and I finished nine texts that nobody was ever going to read.

That became my life for the following months.

*

"WHO DOES HE THINK HE IS? A WALKING SHITBAG! THAT'S WHAT HE IS. HE IS JUST A FETID SHITBAG. I WISH I COULD WIPE OFF THAT SMIRK OF HIS. ASSHOLE. I FUCKING HATE HIM. I HATE HIM! I HATE HIM! I FUCKING HATE HIM! ASSHOLE, ASSHOLE, ASSHOLE. FAT RANCID PIG."

Lucia was not fond of Kaspar's management style, and that didn't take me long to realize.

In turn, talking to that emaciated woman with unkempt black and grey hair was not a pleasant task for Kaspar either. His life revolved around beautiful things: clothes, watches, cars, perhaps beautiful women or men. Each time I saw the dismay filling Kaspar's face, looking at those big glasses leaning on that pointy nose, and those massive eye bags.

Angela, who was Lucia's right arm in the Italian team, nodded at Lucia's venting. Angela always had that apathetic stare into space. She didn't speak to people. She didn't even breathe for all I knew. She was just there and she was the only person in the office Lucia tolerated.

"But we are almost on plan. What did he say?" Angela said.

"He says the other markets have grown more than us this year and he might take a drastic decision on the Italian market," Lucia said.

"He wants to shut down the Italian market?"

"Yes. If we don't reach our quarter goals."

"Son of a bitch."

It was the first time they had invited me and Massimo for a cigarette break. Massimo was not even a smoker, he did it to fit in. Massimo and I smoked and didn't speak unless they asked us something, which happened once.

"So, tell us," Lucia said with a bored expression, "are you guys seeing anyone?"

"I'm single," Massimo said with his usual dignified look.

"Mothers and fathers of Berlin, lock up your daughters," Lucia sneered. She had a smothered laughter. Massimo's eyes darkened as he kept smoking his cigarette.

"What about you?" Lucia asked me.

"I live with my girlfriend," I said, then turned to Massimo and saw him giving me a worried look.

"Is she Italian too?" she asked me.

"She is from Berlin but her father is Italian."

Lucia went on smoking as if all of a sudden she had lost interest in the two of us.

"The new delivery guy is hot," Lucia said to Angela, "did you see those arms? I want to ride him like a raging bitch. I need someone to fuck me good," she cried.

Angela exhaled smoke and kept staring into space.

Later that day Lucia called me, "can you please come over, Tony?" without looking up from her screen.

I stood up and noticed she was reading one of the texts I had written. "Do you think this is a good copy?" she asked.

"Is there something wrong?" I asked. I thought it was better than most of the other texts I had read, but of course I didn't tell her.

"How many times did I tell you to use the keywords?"

"Three times," I said, pointing at each keyword. "One, two, three. There you go!"

She took a deep breath. "I said AT LEAST three times." She looked at me as if she was looking at some crazy man on the verge of ruining her team, her life, the entire company with his careless behavior. "It means you have to use them more than three times."

"Will do," I said.

For some reason, me dealing with her scolding with that *will do* made her snap. Her voice trembled. "Listen, Tony. I don't give a flying shit about syntax and fancy words, just use the fucking keywords as I said."

This time I kept my mouth shut and returned to my desk. Massimo gave me a sympathetic look. "What a bitch," he whispered.

Then it occurred to me that my main concern at that particular moment was to write an article about espadrilles. That kind of struck me in the face. Would have that helped me win Lucia's trust and secure me a contract in that place, anyway? Surely, she was the only person in that company who could influence my career advancement. We were four interns, and I assumed that all of them wrote those eight texts, and some probably more, because they wanted to prove their motivation to their manager. I always assumed other people were more motivated than me.

"Hey Tony," I saw Eva walking to my desk.

"Hi Eva."

"Do you mind throwing out the garbage before you leave?"

Then the cold arrived. I mean, the cold arrived in November and lasted throughout December. What came after was something different. At first I didn't take Marina's warnings seriously. "I will just wear another layer," I kept saying to her and she would look at me in dismay.

Then one day the thermometer hit minus 13 degrees Celsius, and I thought this is not something a person who has spent most of his life in the Mediterranean climate should be allowed to experience. Only after the index and middle fingers of my left hand had acquired a purplish tone and had become coarse to the touch, I figured it was time to buy gloves and a scarf.

One of those days, Eva walked to our desks holding a small framed picture in one hand.

We all kept our eyes down on the screen. The typing intensified. That week, twice I'd had to build a desk for the executives, one time I had to load the dishwasher after lunch, and another time I went to throw out the garbage. For some reason, Massimo and I carried out these duties more than the others.

As Eva approached Lucia, Lucia, after scrutinizing me and Massimo, pointed at him.

Massimo kept staring at his computer screen for a few seconds, then stood up with a jolt and walked off to the meeting room.

"There will be a desk too…" Eva pointed at me, this time without asking Lucia.

"Sure," I stood up and followed her.

"The picture goes on that wall," Eva said to Massimo as we got to the meeting room.

Massimo hammered the nail after trying to discern the exact spot Eva had pointed with her bony finger. He then proceeded to hang the picture on it.

"This is not straight," Eva said. I was across the room, assembling the desk.

Massimo steered the frame of the picture with both hands, attempting to make it straight. Eva still didn't seem pleased. She stood there staring at him with her arms folded. He was hunched, trying his best, but he couldn't put that thing straight.

"Does that seem straight to you?"

Massimo didn't say a word. He was sweating and attempted to reposition the frame.

"Nein! Nein!"

"It is straight, Tony?" he asked me. "Doesn't it seem straight to you?"

I moved a few steps toward them. "It looks straight to me," I said.

Eva gave me a piercing look. "It is not straight," she growled.

"Why don't you do it then?" Massimo twitched and stood up.

I left the unfinished desk on the floor and stood there.

Without a word, Eva walked out of the room. Massimo looked at me as if to ask me what was happening.

All I could answer him with was a shrug.

In about a minute, the door opened. Eva entered, Kaspar was right behind her.

"What's going on here?" He looked at Massimo.

"Look," Massimo waved his arms, "I have been trying to hang this thing for almost half an hour. To me this looks straight. There is nothing wrong with it."

Eva was standing right behind Kaspar with her arms folded. Without looking at the picture, Kaspar began screaming at Massimo. "Now you hang that fucking thing and you do it well."

Massimo just stood there looking at him. "I won't do it!" he said.

Kaspar's face darkened. "THE FUCK DO YOU MEAN YOU WON'T DO IT?!" He looked even bigger than usual. For a moment I thought he would grab Massimo and shatter the glass wall by throwing his body at it.

"You find someone else to do it," Massimo said.

Kaspar pointed his finger at him and screamed, "THEN GET OUT. YOU'RE DONE HERE."

Massimo hollered something in Italian, which I understood but they clearly didn't, walked to his desk, grabbed his jacket, and left for good.

He was replaced by another intern within two days.

Some days later Lucia informed me that she didn't intend to offer me a contract. "There are three other people writing loads of articles and doing extra hours every day. What makes you think I would offer a contract to you?" she said with her usual tenderness.

That same evening I had my laptop on the couch. I rolled a joint and began searching on the Internet for any job or internship in the Berlin metropolitan area that required the Italian language. I didn't bother to read the job descriptions or the information about the company. The fact that they were looking for native Italian speakers was all I needed.

I kept sending the same resume which fit in less than one A4 page and a cover letter, changing in the latter only the recipient information.

In one evening I sent fourteen job applications. The first rejection email arrived the day after.

The rejections did not discourage me. You can't be lucid enough to get discouraged when your best life prospect is to hop from a 400-euro internship to another 400-euro internship. That looked like everything Berlin had to offer to a twenty-four-year-old Italian who didn't speak German and had no actual experience in digital marketing.

That heavy slithering rattle echoed through the night.

I woke up and reached for Marina. Her side of the bed was empty. A sudden chill ran down my spine and I realized I was shivering.

Another rattle shook the walls and the ceiling.

"Marina," I shouted but no one answered.

The window of the bedroom was open. I looked out. The lights of all the buildings were off; Berlin was asleep except for one dim light coming from a building right in front of ours.

Strangely enough, only then I realized that the building mirrored ours. The window with the dim light stood at the same level of our apartment. I took a better look. A man appeared from that window. He was smoking a cigarette and looked in my direction. *How could he see me with the light in my room off?*

He looked at me and smoked with a manic expression on his face.

From my window I saw trees swinging madly as if something was crawling its way and thrusting them aside.

I closed the window and walked to the living room. I then tried looking in the kitchen and the bathroom but found no trace of Marina. I took my jacket and walked down to the courtyard.

"Marina," I shouted, only to realize that the rattling had become more intense.

I returned inside and searched again in every room. *Maybe she left with her phone*, I thought.

I walked back to the bedroom to get my phone but flinched as I reached the door.

On the bed a figure snuggled under the quilt and was peacefully resting on their side, facing the window.

I got closer and noticed a dark head of hair coming out from the blankets.

"Marina," I called for her as I reached for the bed. As I placed one hand on the quilt, the figure rolled in my direction.

I let out a scream as I realized it was not Marina.

"What are you doing here?" I screamed as Lucia pushed the quilt away, revealing her gaunt nudity.

"Fuck me, Tony," she said stretching her arms in my direction. "I just need a good fuck."

"Get out," I screamed and stepped back. Then I heard the door of the bedroom being slammed behind me.

I turned and Eva stood there wearing her usual business suit. "Why does it have to be a big deal, Tony?"

"Where is Marina?" I screamed as the rattle was now coming from inside the building and had become unbearable.

"Do you want us to offer you a contract?" Eva asked me as she held a woven bag. "Think of it. You will have a real salary. No more desks to build. You won't be a slave anymore. Isn't it what you always wanted? After all, don't we all deserve a good fuck now and then?"

"Get out or I'll call the police," I said as the entire place began to shake and a madding, shrill roar ascended, as if someone was dragging a piano through the staircase.

They sneered while Eva reached for the content of the woven bag with one hand and took out a severed head. I recognized it, it was Massimo's. She pointed it at me. "Do you want to end up like him?"

"I am going to call the police." I ran out of the bedroom. They didn't try to stop me and kept sneering.

I made it to the front door. I opened it. I saw it. It was waiting for me.

Then everything went black.

*

It happened on a day in late February. I was at work. I opened my inbox and found an email from Rita Dong from a company named The Dancing Avocado. They had developed an app that evaluated the outfits of its users. You installed the app, took a picture of yourself, and if the algorithm liked your outfit, an anthropomorphic avocado gave you a thumbs up, while if it didn't, the avocado would give you a thumbs down and a look of disapproval.

Rita Dong invited me to their office in Kreuzberg to have an interview with the founder Lukas Voigt. I called myself sick at work and went.

Rita welcomed me at the door. The office was the same size as the one of Go-Go Fashion, but was shared with another startup named Re-Juvinator that had something to do with beauty products. As a matter of fact, I never quite understood what they sold.

Rita asked me to wait in a small lobby surrounded by plants. The place was crowded. There was movement in the hallway and in the glass-walled meeting rooms.

I sat on a chair waiting for the interview with the CEO and leafed through a German magazine about entrepreneurship. An article showed two smiling guys with a close shave and hair combed backwards, both wearing white shirts. They looked alike, except one was skinny and the other fatter. I couldn't understand much of what was written, but I figured the two were brothers.

A lanky man with a beer belly approached me. "Hi Antonio, I am Lukas Voigt." He had a gentle face and asked me to follow him to one of the glass-walled meeting rooms, where he began introducing the company to me.

"I see on your resume you have been developing some SEO skills in your current company," he said.

"The time at Go-Go Fashion has been incredibly valuable," I said.

"May I ask you why you want to leave them?"

"Although I will always be grateful to Kaspar and Benjamin for the opportunity—"

"I know Benjamin. Great guy, isn't he?" By the expression on his face I thought his remark was not genuine.

"He is. You see, I have realized it is time for me to engage in new projects and develop my skills." I paused, waiting for any reaction on his face to tell me if I was pushing the right buttons.

"Do you have experience with link-building?" he asked me.

"No."

"What about Google Analytics?"

"A bit," I said.

"Have you ever worked with it?"

"Not really."

"Tell me about your tasks at Go-Go Fashion."

"I spend most of the time writing product descriptions. I need to optimize each text for a keyword."

"Do you like writing?"

"I do."

"Do you see yourself working in digital marketing in five years?"

"Absolutely."

He gave me a puzzled look.

"Can you tell me more about your marketing strategy?" I asked him. The day before I had read somewhere that it was a good question to ask when one doesn't know much about the business of a company.

"Our strategy consists mostly of testimonial marketing. Are you familiar with it?"

I said yes.

"We give a free trial of The Dancing Avocado app to our testimonials, and in return they promote us on their blogs and social media channels."

I nodded. "What kind of testimonials?"

"Mostly fashion bloggers. We also got on board some minor celebrities. Do you know Franka Steinmeier?"

I said no.

"Thanks for the pleasant chat, Tony. You will hear from us."

I received a call the day after from Rita. I was at work. I rushed to the bathroom and picked up.

"We are happy to offer you a six months internship at The Dancing Avocado. Would you still be interested?"

"Absolutely. Thank you for the opportunity, Rita."

"Also, we would like to invite you to our next Friday Open Bar."

"What's that?"

"Every Friday from 5 pm we throw a party in the office. It could be an opportunity for you to get to meet your new colleagues."

"Count me in, Rita".

I went on Friday after work. I stayed for a few hours, talked to a few people, pretended to enjoy myself and left. Then Marina and I spent the entire weekend between the couch and the bed, except on Saturday night we went to a Vietnamese restaurant in Mitte, ate, and returned straight home.

The following Monday I sent Lucia an email.

Dear Lucia,

I hope this email finds you in good spirits.

I regret to inform you that last Friday was my last day at Go-Go Fashion.

The reason is that I have found another job that I believe is a better fit for my skills and ambitions.
I am available to come to the office to resign from my position or if you prefer to send me the termination document, I can sign it and send it back to you. That's an option too.

I hope you understand. Many thanks for the great opportunity and I wish Go-Go Fashion the best for the future.

Sincerely,
Tony

I went back to bed and snuggled up to Marina.

"So, you will simply stop going?" she asked.

"If I have to stand those faces one day longer, I swear I will cry."

"Can you do that? I mean, isn't there some notice period you have to stick to?"

"Like they give two shits about what's in the contract," I said.

"You want to go visit that apartment in Friedrichshain with me then?"

"When is the guy returning from Brazil?"

"1st of April. We should free the apartment before then."

"Sure," I said. "We could have breakfast at the bar down the street."

"I'll shower first," she said and walked off to the bathroom.

"Wake me up if I fall asleep," I shouted, not sure she heard.

I closed my eyes. A fifteen minute nap would do me good, I thought.

Then my phone rang. It was Lucia. She was mad.

"What do you mean you're not coming anymore?" she squawked.

"I have explained it in the email," I said with a drowsy voice.

"Listen. I expect you to come here right away."

"I have told you I quit."

"Do you realize how unprofessional this is? You can't just stop showing up at work. You could incur a fine for this."

"I won't accept being called unprofessional. I have always behaved exemplarily toward you and the company and done my work despite the time wasted assembling tables and carrying out those humiliating tasks."

She went silent. I wasn't sure if it was from my sudden burst of self-preservation or my insolence.

"Listen, Tony," her tone became more reconciling, "do you understand that you signed a contract and everyone who intends to quit must stick to a notice period?"

"You said that you didn't intend to prolong my contract anyway," I said.

"Come to the office and we will talk about it."

I was there thirty minutes later. As she saw me entering, Lucia walked to the HR office to call Eva.

Eva invited me to follow the two of them into a room.

"Your contract reads that you must give us a one month notice period. You can't just walk away like this," Eva said.

"Lucia said she didn't intend to extend my contract here one month ago. Do you expect me to sit and wait until I become jobless?"

"You have to comply with what you signed on the contract when you started here. You're putting Lucia in an uncomfortable situation," Eva said.

"Well, on that contract I read nothing about assembling desks or throwing out the garbage. And I have done it almost every day for the last four months," I said.

Eva's look turned into a mix of outrage and disbelief. She didn't reply.

"Do not expect that in your next company it will be different. Are you really that naïve to believe that?" Lucia said angrily. "As long as you are an intern, they will always ask you to carry out these tasks. And do not expect that after your six months internship they will make you CEO either." That mockery must have given her courage, I thought.

They both stared at me, waiting for my surrender.

It was like reality had just smacked my face. I was just a foreigner who didn't speak the local language and didn't know anyone in town, against a Platypusnetic company. Even if I was that desperate to take legal action, how many chances did I have against them?

"Look," I said, "it took me time to find this job. If I give it up, it could take months to find another one. How much time do you need to find a replacement for me? One week? Not even. What about Massimo?

It took you two days to find a replacement for him.”

Eva’s arms were crossed. She glanced at me, then at Lucia. “All right, let’s meet halfway. What if you keep coming for the next two weeks?” she asked me.

“That’s fine for me,” I said.

“Would that work for you?” she asked Lucia.

“Fine. But on the condition that you write at least twelve texts every day,” she said to me. She had no guts to go against Eva.

In those two remaining weeks I wrote twelve texts every working day. That made 120 texts that nobody was ever going to read. They never asked me to assemble chairs or desks, nor to empty or load the dishwasher. I had to inform Rita that I would start one week late and was worried that it would have made them change their minds on hiring me. Fortunately, that didn’t happen.

On my last day at Go-Go Fashion, Benjamin walked to my desk and handed me a bottle of Rotkäppchen, an Eastern German sparkling wine. “Good luck, Antonio. And thanks for everything,” he said with his blaring voice and a crooked effort of a smile with those massive incisors.

On the first day at The Dancing Avocado we all stood in a meeting room, forming a circle for what they called the weekly round-up. It was hot in that room, despite it being still early March, and the sunlight flooded the room, passing through the window wall that looked out on the Spree River.

In those meetings each team leader had five minutes to share with the rest the biggest achievements and challenges they'd faced in the previous week.

The Spanish team went first. The German, the Dutch, the Italian, and the French followed. Each of their representatives gave a speech.

In some cases Lukas and his co-founder Marcus would barge in with questions or remarks.

Marcus Kranz was a platinum blond skinny guy who was one year older than me but The Dancing Avocado was already the second company under his name. He was born somewhere in the south of Germany and spent part of his life in Stockholm, where he had founded an online dating website with another guy. The company didn't survive its first year and he returned to Germany where he founded The Dancing Avocado.

It was the turn of the American team. Its representative was a girl named Ashley. She spoke slowly as she reported the numbers achieved during the week.

"Is this a joke?" Marcus interrupted her. "These numbers are a disgrace," he yelled. He had frantic eyes.

Ashley stared at her feet as Marcus kept screaming at her, threatening that the company would stop sponsoring her working visa and other nasty things. She covered her mouth with a hand, trying to contain the sobs, but she couldn't hold it and burst into a crying jag.

Marcus turned his attention to the next speaker while people in the room attempted to comfort the American girl. A girl stretched her arm around her shoulders as Ashley kept sobbing before they left the room together.

Joe was next. He was the head of the British team, the most profitable at that moment. Having concluded the week with a new record in profit, after his speech, the room burst into applause.

Then Rita asked the new employees, me included, to introduce themselves to the rest of the company. There was one guy from Spain, one from the US and a girl from the Netherlands.

"I am Hector, from Andalusia."

"I am Chris, from California, and I can't wait to work with you all."

I was the third. "I am Tony, from Italy. It's great to be here." Marcus still had that crazed look in his eyes as we spoke.

It was the Dutch girl's turn. "Hi everyone..." As she began to introduce herself we heard a thud.

Everyone turned to the source of it. Ashley, who in the meantime had returned to the meeting, lay flat on her back, passed out.

Marcus rushed to her aid. "Bring some water," he hollered.

The girl revived after a few seconds, then stood up with Marcus still clutching her arm and smiled timidly.

Marcus let her go and walked out of the room. Ashley stood there for a few seconds, disoriented, with two people holding her up as we all returned to work.

After the meeting Rita approached me. "Hi, Tony. Would you mind helping the others assemble some desks?"

"Sure," I said with a smile but in my head I screamed in horror at the thought of Lucia's words when I announced my intention to leave Go-Go Fashion. She was right. As long as I was an intern, nothing could have saved me from assembling one or two desks when needed. Perhaps she had put some sort of spell on me.

"It will be only for today," Rita said charmingly.

Two other newbies had already started as I joined them. Chris, the newly arrived in the American team, was a short guy with straight dark hair and bulging eyes. He wore an earring in his left ear and, no matter what he was doing, he kept talking. The other was Hector, from Spain.

"I lived in Florence for one year," Chris said. "My Italian is not too bad. You need to speak and not worry about making mistakes if you want to practice a new language. Do you speak German?" he asked me.

"I don't," I said.

"You should speak it whenever you have the occasion. You oughtn't be shy… Dude, you're screwing it too tight," he warned me as I worked on my desk. "It will crack… look at that…"

His voice broke as a girl who worked for Re-Juvinator, our neighbor company, walked through the shared hallway, carrying a drum full of water with one hand. That thing must have weighed about 15 kilos. She wore a pair of leggings and a tank top that highlighted her prominent breasts. Her left arm was clinched holding the drum in a display of muscle definition. She strode through, leaning on her right side to counterbalance the weight of the drum, with her golden ponytail hanging and showing her slim neck.

Hector dropped the screwdriver which made a hollow sound as it fell on the wood of the desk. Chris stopped talking. *That woman is the only person in the office able to shut him up*, I thought.

"Look at that," Chris whispered.

My desk was ready. Months of practice paid off.

*

In late March, a few days before Marina and I had to free the apartment in Neukölln, we went to visit a place in a *Hinterhaus* in the Wedding District. It was a 50-square-meter unfurnished apartment with a small kitchen, living room and bedroom. The bathroom had a bathtub.

The owner was a man in his fifties, the *Berliner Schnauze* type. He talked only to Marina after she told him I didn't speak German. As they talked, he kept looking at me with startled eyes.

"I am looking for quiet people," he said to Marina. "You can invite people and occasionally throw parties, but please be respectful of the neighbors."

She translated to me.

"Right on," I said and he gave me another startled look.

They seemed to enjoy their conversation. A real Berliner would hardly find pleasure in small talk, unless he met another Berliner. Make no mistake, I hardly grasped a tenth of what they talked about. I always assumed they made the typical Berliner jokes, as if to prove they carry the proper Berliner wit. It is like, 'You are from Berlin, how many generations? Oh yeah? Me too, I'll show you', and then they go on complaining about the things real Berliners complain about, mainly gentrification and the increasing cost of rents.

As Marina kept talking to the guy, I looked through a window that looked onto a park that flanked the backyard. A woman was walking her two dogs. One of them pooped next to a bench. The woman took a plastic bag from the pocket of her loose jacket and picked up the excrement.

"What do you think?" Marina asked me as we left the apartment.

"I like it," I said, "it's spacious."

"Me too," Marina said, "it's just that…"

"What?"

"Well, it's Wedding," she said.

"What's wrong with Wedding?" I had never heard of a Berlin district named Wedding before visiting the apartment. "I like it in here, it's colorful. Besides, look at how many interesting people there are." I pointed at a guy seated on a bench reading a book. He must have been about sixty, with unkept beard and stormy grey hair. He was tall and wore a tattered grey suit that was one size too small. The book looked minuscule in his massive hands.

"He looks like some cursed poet or something," Marina said.

"I bet he is."

"Should we just take the apartment?"

"Why not? Also the landlord seems like an affable guy."

"He does."

"Have I told you about my colleague Hector?"

"The Spaniard?"

"Yes, the other day we were talking about rents and he told me that some months ago he had found a nice shared apartment in Kreuzberg. He was not working at The Dancing Avocado yet."

"What a ridiculous name for a company."

"They all have ridiculous names. Anyway, the room was spacious and at walking distance from work. The catch was that his flat-mate and landlord was convinced he was being spied on by the Spanish intelligence."

"Why did he think that?"

"No idea, he kept begging Hector to keep the blinds shut on weekdays. On the weekends and bank holidays it was fine though. Hector didn't mind at first. 'He is a brilliant guy,' he kept saying when he told me about his landlord."

"What happened?"

"One night he broke into Hector's room. He wore nothing except his boxer and socks and was wrapped up in a quilt.

'THEY ARE HERE!' He swung Hector's window open and started screaming like a madman. 'I KNOW YOU'RE HERE, SONS OF BITCHES. WHAT DO YOU WANT? YOU HAVE NOTHING AGAINST ME. YOU CAN SUCK MY DICK!' And he took the thing out of his boxers and began swinging it at the window."

"Are you sure your colleague didn't make it up?"

"Why would he? Wait, there is more."

"Oh God…"

"At that particular moment Hector was not alone on his bed but with a colleague of his he had been craving to date for months."

"Poor girl. Are they still seeing each other?"

"I didn't ask him that."

"But why on earth would the Spanish intelligence have interest in his landlord?"

"He doesn't know either."

We got the apartment and rented a small van to transport our belongings, mainly Marina's. In the first month we slept on a couch bed that was in Marina's room at her parents' house. Every night we wondered what was the squeak coming from the apartment above. It had regular intervals, like those of a pendulum. Sometimes we heard screams coming from the same apartment.

In the building there were low-income families for the most part, mostly Turkish, and some young couples and people living alone. Kids played red light-green light in the courtyard while their mums with their hijabs sat on the benches smoking. The children greeted us, danced and sang as we walked by, while the mothers pretended not to see us.

The other member of the Italian team was Monica. Monica had started the Italian market from scratch and it occurred to me she acted quite jealousy about it. For some reason, she kept making awkward jokes, and she alone laughed at them.

"Did you bold the text?… Did you use the keyword at least three times?… What about those links?" she asked every couple of hours.

She was all for pinpointing errors and seemed concerned I would fuck up everything if she let down her guard.

"I have used the keyword four times, everything should be fine, have a look yourself."

"Let me see," she said behind those coke-bottle glasses and thick curls that fell on the frame. "It looks good this time. Please avoid the mistakes you made the other day."

A few days earlier I had forgotten to bold some sections of a text and she accused me of being distracted and began telling me off as if I were some high school student in need of a good scolding. Monica was two years younger than me.

"I will, thanks for your feedback, Monica," I said.

"Otherwise I will have to fire you," she said.

I looked at her, confused.

"I am kidding," she giggled. "I can't fire you because I am not your boss."

There was a sense of awkwardness each time I had to talk to her and she didn't seem enthusiastic about sharing her raft with another person.

"Can you show me that vlookup function on Excel?" I asked her after a while, "Quique showed me the other day but I'm afraid I'm not doing it right."

"You better ask him again or Joe."

I walked to Joe's desk. "Hey Joe, could you help me with something?"

"Hey fag, what's up?" Joe was from Liverpool and, for some reason, he kept making jokes implying the homosexuality of his male interlocutors. Despite that he was of the nice sort. Whenever I had some issues that Monica could not help me with, I went to him. He helped on the spot, without acting judgmental or annoyed. I liked Joe.

"Could you show me the vlookup function? I can't do it right."

"Sure."

I sat next to him and he opened an empty Excel sheet where he recreated the function for me to take note.

"Thanks, Joe. You're a good lad," I said.

He then mumbled something. I often had a hard time understanding his tight Northern English accent.

"What?"

Incomprehensible Northern English mumbling.

"Again?"

INCOMPREHENSIBLE NORTHERN ENGLISH MUMBLING.

"What?"

"OH, PISS OFF!"

I pissed off.

That Friday at 5 pm sharp they brought six ice boxes stuffed with beer bottles. Most people pounced on them like thirsty hyenas, while the interns were more cautious.

Two guys and a girl from Re-Juvinator were talking to Lukas.

Except for Lukas and Marcus, the Re-Juvinator folks didn't interact much with the people from The Dancing Avocado. They were for the most part Germans and looked like most people think Germans should look. They dressed differently than us too. The men wore perfectly ironed shirts, usually white or pastel colors. They were tall, short, fat, skinny, fit, but they all wore those pastel shirts in the same way, cuffing the sleeves at the wrists on warmer days. For some reason, they all had that slicked back hairstyle, shorter on the back and on the sides. They looked down on us. They didn't talk to us and we didn't talk to them. We tried our best to tolerate each other and to avoid stepping on each other's toes.

Anna, the woman I'd seen carrying the water drum on my first day, joined them. Marcus joined soon after and began following her everywhere she went.

Hector walked to my desk; he was drinking a beer and handed me another.

"You got yourself a new boyfriend?" Joe said to Hector as he walked past my desk with his backpack.

"What's up, Italiano?" he asked me. "Are your faggot bosses treating you well?"

"What's up Joe? I can't complain," I answered.

"You guys are being enslaved by those two sons of a bitch. You have all the reasons to complain. Welcome to the freakshow!" He chuckled and began walking to the door.

"Aren't you staying for a beer?" Hector asked him.

"Naa… Liverpool are playing tonight and I need to put my son to sleep before then. See you on Monday, fags."

"See you Joe."

Soon everyone in the office had gone on a drinking spree. The bulk was at the lobby, where people sat on the sofas, and in the office kitchen where Quique of the Spanish team was distributing cinnamon and lime slices for a round of tequila. In the kitchen they were listening to reggaeton music.

When I entered, Quique was pouring the cinnamon on the base of the thumbs of the people that were forming a circle. There was a method in the way he did it, like a minister distributing the host to the worshippers who patiently waited for their turn.

"Take a shot glass, *cabron*!" he screamed at me.

Quique was in charge of the Spanish team and had reached legendary status within the company. Whatever the occasion, he enjoyed drinking more than most of our colleagues. He was yet to turn thirty but was stout and already partially bald and despite that, he was popular among the ladies too. He was one of the top performers of the company and always showed up on time, even when he had spent the night before drinking, which was often the case.

I gulped the tequila, sucked the cinnamon, and bit the lime slice.

Ashley from the American team approached me. "Come sing at karaoke!"

"Give a glass to the American woman," ordered Quique to someone in the crowd. She took the glass and emptied it.

"We are going to play The Killers!" she screamed in my ear. She then said something that I couldn't understand and left. The loud reggaeton music didn't help the cause.

"Tony, do you like football?" Juan, our front-end developer, approached me.

"I do," I said.

"What's your team?"

"I don't have a team."

"What do you watch football for?" He laughed.

"It soothes me," I said.

"Messi or Ronaldo?" he asked.

"Messi," I said.

"Correct," he said. "We are going to smoke *un porro* downstairs. Wanna join?"

I asked what that was.

"A joint," he smirked. "Want to come with us?"

We went down to the backyard where Juan lit the joint. Hector and Quique joined too.

"Man, that Anna is illegal," said Quique as he passed the joint around. He had switched to English because of me.

"*Joder*," said Hector. "Marcus is in full hunting mode today."

"I didn't even think he could have a hard on," Juan said.

"Perhaps he is into bondage," Quique said, "taking pleasure only from pain".

"I bet he is," Juan said.

"She should choose me. I am as plain as a guy can get in bed," said Quique. We laughed and Juan made a choking sound as he inhaled the smoke.

"But to be honest," Quique added, "I think he likes money more than anything."

"What about Lukas? You have known him for a while," asked Hector. "*Hombre*, I have a hard time understanding how these two could run a business together."

"I began working with Lukas in his previous company, about two years ago," said Quique. "Marcus arrived last year and they founded The Dancing Avocado. They asked me to take over the Spanish market."

"How did Lukas and Marcus meet?" I asked.

"Through an investor in Lukas's previous company," said Quique. "He had told Lukas about this talented guy who worked in Stockholm back then and had them meet. He thought that Marcus's entrepreneurial skills and Lukas's knowledge in web development and digital marketing was a good combination. So they founded The Dancing Avocado."

"I bet Lukas makes only cyber-sex," said Juan.

"Germany's best cyber-lover," Hector said. The others laughed.

As we returned upstairs, Ashley approached again. "Come sing karaoke!"

She clutched and pressed my elbow against her breast before handing me a glass. It contained rum and something else. I gulped it and entered the meeting room where Monica and another girl were singing and other people were drinking. Leaning against the wall next to the door were two guys from Re-Juvinator, sneering at them. Monica and her companion didn't seem to notice and kept singing.

As I left the meeting room, Chris waved a bottle of vodka at me. I drank from it, and he invited me to join a group of people sitting in the lobby. I sat with them as they drank and chatted. They began asking me questions.

"Where are you from in Italy?"

I answered.

"Oh…" That was usually the reaction.

"How long have you been in Berlin?"

"Do you like it here?"

"I love it!" I said.

Quique brought another bottle of tequila and screamed at someone in the crowd, "We are running out of beer!

"Italiano," he yelled at me. He had a genuine smile despite the liters of booze he had already gulped that night. It was easy to understand why everyone was fond of him in that company. "Go check in the storage room if those stingy motherfuckers have hidden some bottles."

There was one door that flanked the main entrance and a smaller one between the kitchen and the men's bathroom. One led to the storage room while the other to the server room, although I didn't know which one belonged to which.

I tried with the smaller one and got it on the first try. That looked like a storage room. However, as I opened it, I saw Marcus's back with his pants lying on the floor. Beyond his hunched figure Ashley, the American girl, was surrounding his waist with her legs.

I shut the door. There was no crate of beer in there.

I checked the server room just in case, but all I saw were cables and circuits. Go figure what I was expecting to find in there.

Empty handed, I followed Quique and the others to the kitchen where we had two more rounds of tequila.

After a while, Ashley arrived and grabbed my arm again. "Let's go sing karaoke," she screamed. She must haven't noticed me before in the storage room. She was drunk and Chris stood next to her.

Chris was born in San Diego, a second generation Mexican. He was twenty-eight, older than most of the other interns. That helped him on the job. He was not afraid to speak in front of the entire team during the weekly round-ups. He took the job seriously and one could tell he was an ambitious fella. Some said Chris bragged a lot, but no one denied he was of a nice sort.

He stood there staring at Ashley. I got the feeling he favored blond women. He was drunk, drunker than me, and his eyes seemed somewhat less bulging. He held an almost empty bottle of vodka in his hand but he acted as if he had forgotten about it.

I left Chris and Ashley, went down to the backyard on my own, and lit a cigarette. The booze and the marijuana were kicking in, and I thought some fresh air would help me sober up. It must have been past midnight; there was no one else in the backyard. It was a night in early April. It was chilly outside, but in Berlin the air in spring smelled differently than in winter, I thought. Or perhaps I was just high.

The wooden door that led to the inner building opened and Anna, the water drum girl, came out.

She saw me and smiled. "Got a light?" She asked.

I handed her a lighter.

She grabbed a pack from the pocket of her blazer. "Shit, I'm out of cigarettes," she groaned.

"Here you go," I said, handing her my pack. It felt light in my hand.

"But you have one left."

"I had enough for today. This job makes me smoke too much," I said.

"The job or all the partying going on?" She smirked.

"It seems they go hand-in-hand," I said.

"Tell me about it. We should cut this stuff out," she said.

"You mean the job or the cigarettes?" I asked and that made her laugh.

"Are you having a good time?" she asked.

"I am," I said.

She gave me a doubtful look. "Where are you from?" she asked.

I told her. "Where are you from?" I asked her.

"I was born in Köln, but my mother is Dutch. Are you really having a good time?"

"Sure," I said. "Well, I am not much of a party guy. More like a stay-at-home type. But I am enjoying my time."

"I'm a big couch potato too," she said candidly. "We are in the wrong place."

"It could be worse than this," I grinned. We studied each other for a few seconds, not saying a word. Surely, she didn't strike me as someone distant from social events, but perhaps she thought the same about me. "What do you do?" I asked.

"I am in charge of marketing. I started as an intern five months ago, then they offered me to take over the marketing and here I am. What is that you do?"

"You know what? I am still trying to figure it out," I said.

She laughed and right at that moment someone swung the door open. Marcus came out of it furiously. He gave me a murderous look then directed his frantic eyes to Anna. "I need to talk to you," he said in German. At least that was what I understood. He always had that demanding tone.

She said something back, still smiling. I kept smoking my cigarette. She seemed annoyed by that tone of his; I couldn't tell for sure. Her gaze was lost in space while she inhaled the smoke. Then he said something else. This time his tone was softer as if he was imploring her.

"Okay," she said and began walking away. He trotted behind her, like a lap dog that happily follows its master after having taken a shit in the streets.

She then turned to me. "Have a good night," she said, smiling.

Marcus stopped walking, turned, and gave me another murderous look before hastening his pace to catch up with her.

In May more people joined the company, including a girl from Italy. Her name was Adriana. With Adriana, we were now three in the Italian team and Monica seemed even less pleased.

"She detests me," Adriana told me the first week. "She keeps scolding me for no reason. And, Tony, I don't want to sound mean," she paused, "but have you noticed how ugly she is?"

Good thing for me was that since Adriana's arrival, Monica had stopped being a pain in my ass.

"She is just tense as her contract is ending," I said.

"Has she spoken to Marcus and Lukas for the renewal?"

"They always tell her they haven't made a decision yet. The first time she requested a meeting was in March, I had just started then."

The following week, Monica finally had the meeting with Lukas she had been requesting.

Lukas told her that she was no longer needed in the Italian team. When she returned from the meeting, she grabbed her things, hugged a few people, and left for good.

On those days there was a coming and going from Marcus and Lukas's office. They kept calling people from every team, who until that moment were only interns or juniors. Adriana was one of them.

"Do you know what's going on?" Hector asked me with a worried look but I was as clueless as he. Then he turned to Quique. "Quique, *tio*, are we all gonna get fired?"

Quique smiled. "I don't think so," he said, "but something is happening."

That didn't make Hector any less nervous.

"Tony, *hermano*. Your new colleague is hot," he said referring to Adriana.

"Is this why they let Monica go?" Hector sneered.

"Monica too had her qualities," Quique said.

"Shut up," Hector said.

"I'm serious," Quique insisted.

"What do you mean?" Hector asked as if all of a sudden he had stopped being worried.

"I mean she knew one or two things," Quique said, looking at his screen.

"You saying that you and Monica…"

Quique didn't reply. He was still looking at his screen.

"Quique?"

Quique kept looking at the screen.

"Did you or did you not?" Hector asked.

"I did," Quique confessed at last.

"I have got news," Adriana told me after returning to her seat. She had spent almost an hour in Marcus and Lukas's office.

"What's up?"

"Marcus promoted me to team leader of the Italian team."

"This is great, congratulations!" I said.

"I am not sure."

"What's wrong?" I asked her.

"I am not cut out for it. I know nothing about managing people."

"Well, it seems you will be managing me," I said.

Then everything began to make sense. It occurred to me that they had hired me in the first place, hoping that I could be the right replacement for Monica, only to realize that I didn't possess the skills they looked for. That was the reason they kept waiting before giving Monica an answer concerning her renewal. Then came Adriana. Graduated from a good university, good looks, and the outspokenness that every team leader needs. "Son of a bitch," I muttered.

"Who?"

"Never mind," I said. "Adriana, I think you will do great."

"Thanks, Tony. But there is more."

"Uh?"

"I won't be your boss, they have other plans for you."

"What plans?"

The next day they called me and a bunch of people from the other teams to attend a meeting held by Lukas and Marcus. As we entered the meeting room, we found this blond, neat guy no one had seen before.

"You are going to be part of our SEO team," said Lukas. He looked proud as he spoke. "The future of this company is in your hands. This is why we have called Bernhard. He is an SEO expert and will train you for the next three months. He is concluding his bachelor degree at the prestigious Hoffmann University, one of the most selective research institutions in Germany."

Bernhard appeared confident as he introduced himself, although his face betrayed a certain skepticism. As if he was there because he had to be. Or perhaps that was just his normal face.

"Does anyone have questions for Bernhard?" Lukas asked.

Chris raised his hand. "Can you tell us more about the job?"

"You will build links," Bernhard answered. "Google gives more exposure to websites that hold many inbound links, meaning we must make sure that as many websites as possible out there link to us."

"But doesn't Google stigmatize the link-building practice? I read that if they find out we pay for links, we may get a penalty," pointed out Quique. Quique was seated, keeping his arms crossed and glaring at this kid who must have been at least five years younger than him.

"That is correct," said Bernhard who somehow looked more skeptical than Quique.

"What kind of websites should we contact?" Hector asked.

"The same we have been doing business with until now." Bernhard's voice broke up as he turned to the glass wall facing the hallway. The rest followed as Anna walked by and for a few seconds the meeting went silent.

"Fashion blogs," Bernhard uttered at last.

"WE MUST GET MENTIONED BY THE BEST BLOGGERS OUT THERE, THE BEST!" Marcus hollered, seemingly out of context, and proceeded to bang his fist on the desk. He must have considered that a rare showcase of motivational skills as he smiled proudly, before going quiet again.

Both Lukas and Bernhard looked at him in dismay. Bernhard as if he had realized what sort of a nutjob he was working for. Others didn't catch the motivational intent and their faces filled with terror.

I began spending my days sending emails to a bunch of deranged folks who called themselves 'fashion bloggers'. These people, mostly young women but there were a few men too, wore clothes, they took pictures of themselves wearing those clothes, or asked their boyfriends, girlfriends, mothers, or grandmothers to take them, and then they published them on their blogs for the world to see. And I had to talk to these people, as many other companies like ours did to promote their services. There was little to no boundary to the sort of attention-seeking, self-denying looneys we were instructed to contact.

"So you want to write about me on your website. This is so exciting!" one of them said over the phone on one of my first days as an SEO specialist, whatever that meant.

"I am afraid I was not clear. What I proposed to you in the email is to write an article about our app on your blog."

"So, what is it that you want? A link, ehm… what is it exactly? Could you explain how to create it? What's in for me?"

"We would be glad to offer you a free trial for our app or a money transfer."

"I was hoping for more than fifty euros. Jessica from the Passion Fruit Blog told me you paid her seventy-five euros for one article. This is so humiliating. I think I am going to write about your dishonest conducts on my blog."

The following day on her blog she wrote about how horrible we were to take advantage of her, that our company was a scam, and warned other bloggers against responding to our inquiries. Luckily she didn't mention my name but the alias I used. Bernhard had advised the bunch of us to use fake names when dealing with these people. Last thing you want is your name showing in an article written by an eighteen-year-old girl who accuses you of taking advantage of her. At the end of the article she included a picture of herself taken in front of a mirror with a saddened look and her index finger hanging between her pouting lips. She even included a link that pointed to our website, probably without realizing it was exactly what I had asked her for in the first place.

I spent most of my working day looking at those blogs, mainly at their pictures. I skipped the texts as I soon realized how poorly written and filled with cliches they were. I felt a sense of discomfort looking at those images taken in the dusty attics of clueless girls who tried to imitate those who had made it.

To be fair, they were not all that delusional and a few of them knew too well what they were doing. Some realized they could actually make a living out of it, as the first clothing brands began sending them money and clothes to wear for their blog articles. Why would a twenty-something-year old, good-looking, and who lives in some oppressive town in the countryside say no to that money? Some might say it was a degrading expression of our appearance culture, but was it more deplorable than working eight hours a day for a company named The Dancing Avocado, underpaid and for a psychopath who was only one year older than me?

"How was work today?" Marina asked when I returned home.

"I got nine back-links."

"What?"

"Forget it. How was your day?"

Luckily, from then on she stopped asking.

Juan got a spare ticket to Motörhead. He had bought it for his girlfriend but she had to pass due to an unforeseen late shift at her call center job. There is always someone in a worse situation than yours.

I had never been much of a metalhead, but the idea of seeing Lemmy Kilmister in person convinced me, so I gave Juan the thirty-five euros, a special price under the circumstances, and went with him right after work.

It was a venue used for rock and pop concerts. When we got there, people were starting to fill up the place and we made it to the front row. We each got a beer and soon the opening act came on stage, a hard rock band from the US I had never heard of. They played a thirty-minute-something show while their lead guitarist kept pulling heavy riffs and winking at an eye-catching girl who stood next to me.

"I think he is trying to tell you something," I said to the girl.

"Oh Jeff, well… he is a friend of mine," she smiled.

"You have known him for a long time?" I asked her.

"I have been to a couple of his gigs."

"You don't strike me as a metalhead," I said after noticing the white fur gilet she wore that clashed with the surrounding environment.

"Neither do you," she said after taking a good look at my clothes.

When the last song was over, Jeff beckoned the girl to follow him backstage.

"I have to go," she said to me. "Wait. Would you like to meet the band?"

"Thanks, but I don't want to leave my friend alone. Give my regards to Jeff. Tell him it was a fine gig."

She went after him and the lights went on. Juan and I went to take a piss and bought another beer. We waited in front of the stage for a while, then the lights went off again.

A man with a bass guitar emerged from obscurity wearing heavy cowboy boots and the unmistakable cavalry hat. A roar accompanied the entrance of the band.

The mythical presence stood above everyone else in the venue, only a few meters away from us, "Good evening, are you doing alright?" the raspy voice began, before unleashing hell and sending the audience into a frenzy.

"I think we have made a big mistake," Juan yelled in my ear.

"What? Don't tell me you thought we were going to see Rod Stewart."

"We should have worn earplugs. We need earplugs if we want to stand this close," Juan yelled.

"What? Why? They should have at least written it somewhere on the tickets. You know, as a disclaimer for first-timers. Motörhead for Dummies or something like that. Do you want to move a few meters back?"

He looked as if, for a few seconds, he was giving it a thought, then we agreed that hearing damage was worth the stake.

After a few songs, a group of about ten white behemoths with shaved heads emerged from the back rows and gathered below the stage, pushing me, Juan and others in the front a few meters away from the stage. Then, as if under some wicked spell, they began writhing and banging their heads and pouncing on each other with all their body weight. The rest of the audience was not spared as some bystander was violently thrown off their feet and a woman got a bleeding nose. An almost two-meter-tall son of a bitch was thrown over me by an even bigger son of a bitch, but somehow I managed to stand on my feet.

The concert went on undisturbed while they began wrestling on the ground. I stood there trying to enjoy the show, and at the same time not being headbutted on the crotch, when I noticed this guy standing right next to me. A fifty-something wearing a military jacket. He glared at those guys rolling about on the ground as if they were pigs bathing in the mud. Then he looked straight at me in the eyes, and with his hand he mimicked a gun and pretended to shoot the head of a bald guy who wrestled on top of another.

I gave him a nervous smile and went back to watching the show.

When it was over, Juan and I went out and smoked a joint on the sidewalk. "I'm going to pick up my girlfriend at the U-Bahn station. You want to have a beer with us? I know a place across the street."

"Sure, take your time. I will wait here," I said and lit a cigarette as Juan walked away.

I was on my third cigarette when I decided to call Juan. The message told me his phone was unreachable.

Can't blame him for wanting to spend time with his girlfriend, I thought.

I lit another cigarette and began walking to the U-Bahn station. There was quiet as the crowd of the concert had already dispersed. After all, it was still Wednesday. If I made it on time, I could get some good sleep, I thought. Marina should be home any minute after her evening shift at the catering. We could chill for a bit on the couch before going to sleep.

When does this ringing in my ears go away? They should have written somewhere to wear earplugs.

At first I thought it was the ringing, but I heard something coming from a narrow alley. *Should I go check?* The adrenaline of the concert was still kicking in. *Let's go check.*

I walked into the alley, then turned right. Then I wished I hadn't done so.

Four or five of those behemoths that raised hell at the concert lay face down in a pool of blood. Standing next to them, the man with the military jacket who at the concert had mimicked the handgun was intent on cleaning the blood off a survival knife with the ripped Motörhead t-shirt of one of the behemoths.

He noticed me standing at the corner and gave me a nod. *Too bad for them.*

I began running to the U-Bahn in an attempt to get the last train of the day. Took my phone and dialed 110. As I waited for an operator to pick up, a song began playing. It was "Another Day in Paradise" by Phil Collins. Someone picked up. A man. He began speaking German.

"Hi, do you speak English?" I asked.

He said something I couldn't understand.

"Listen," I cried, "there has been a murder. Four men have been killed. There is blood everywhere."

The operator hollered something in German.

"Is there anyone who can speak English? Dude, I saw this guy with a huge knife. You should send someone right away."

The operator began screaming. I couldn't understand anything of what he said but I could tell his tone had become more threatening.

I had almost reached the U-Bahn station. The guy kept screaming then he hung up. "Another Day in Paradise" began playing again.

I checked my call history, thinking I had dialed the wrong number. 110. *Jesus Christ.*

Then everything began to make sense. It was very simple. I was hallucinating. That was it. The four dead behemoths. The man with the military jacket. Phil Collins. I had had a few beers, smoked a joint. Okay, that alone would not explain the hallucinations. Perhaps it was the adrenaline of the concert. What about that ringing in my ear? It might have done some damage to my brain.

I made it to the platform only to find out that the last train of the day had just passed and for the first time I wished I had a smartphone to let Google Maps show me the way home.

I wandered on the scarcely-lit sidewalk without knowing where I was going, until I came across a bunch of people waiting in line to enter what looked like a nightclub. I walked in their direction, hoping that as there were people there should also be a cab somewhere. Some wore little to no clothes, mostly straps that covered the most intimate parts, and waited patiently for the bouncer to let them in. Surely that looked like a cheerful gang.

I was walking past them with my head down when a female voice shouted my name.

"Tony, over here," she shouted in Italian.

I turned around and saw a girl moving a few steps away from the line of people and waving at me. She had a slim silhouette and her hair was tied in a ponytail.

I walked in her direction, "Adri?" I recognized her behind the heavy makeup.

"Tony, what are you doing here?"

"Just taking a stroll."

She laughed. "Here? At this time? Don't you live in Wedding?"

"Well, I was at the Motörhead concert with Juan. Do you know where I can find a cab?"

She laughed. "Come on. I will introduce you to my friends."

"Alright," I said.

We joined the people waiting in line and she introduced her friends to me. They were all Italian. "Good to meet you all" I said.

I felt all the eyes of the other people in line on me.

"Why don't you come with us?" Adriana proposed, all excited.

"I think I have told you I'm not much into clubbing," I said.

"Come on, it will be fun," Adri said.

"Come on," a bearlike friend of hers with a big beard patted vehemently on my shoulder. "You don't want to make Adri sad."

It was almost 2 in the morning and I had already blown my chance to get some decent sleep. "Alright," I said.

"Where does he think he is going?" said someone with a German accent to another.

"Look how he is dressed," said the other and giggled.

I turned around and saw these two guys standing behind me.

"Well, it's my right to keep my ass warm," I said. One of them wore a torn pair of hot-pants that covered very little of his gaunt butt cheeks. "Besides, aren't we here to celebrate diversity?"

"Pff," they both rolled their eyes and looked at each other with an offended expression. "Macho," one of them muttered.

We waited in line for twenty minutes. I grabbed my phone from my pocket to inform Marina, only to realize the battery was dead.

When it was our turn to get in, the bouncer, a scraggy bald guy with eye shadow and a fur shawl, took a good look at me. "He can't come in," he said to Adriana.

"Why not?" Adriana protested.

"Because I say so," the bouncer replied.

"But he is with us. I come here every week. My friends never caused you any trouble," Adriana said.

"Yeah, but guess what, I make the rules, not you, sweetheart. Now you guys are blocking the others. Get in or you may as well fuck off," the bouncer said.

"It's okay with me," I said. "You guys go in and have fun. I'll see you tomorrow, Adri."

"I'm sorry, Tony. It would have been fun."

"Yeah," I said and began to walk away.

"I have told you," the guy behind me with the hot-pants giggled.

"That just made your day, didn't it?" I replied. "Wait a minute. You guys know where I can get a cab?"

"Sure, just go straight ahead and make sure you don't take a wrong turn," they sneered.

"Yeah, whatever," I muttered and began wandering again in the night.

After a while, I noticed a vehicle parked under a S-Bahn bridge. The ringing still in my ears. I got closer and realized it was a cab. I reached for my wallet to see how much I had left. Twelve euros and forty cents. *Is it enough to get home? I might as well ask the driver before getting in.*

The lights of the cab were off and I noticed the driver lying on the reclined seat, watching some video on his smartphone.

I heard gasps and moans coming from his smartphone. In normal circumstances I would have stayed clear. But hey, it was me not having to spend the night on a park bench or this dude getting a good jack off.

I chose me and knocked on the back seat window. I glimpsed the guy bustling to zip his pants and put the seat back straight, then he stuck his face out of the window.

"What do you want?" he muttered.

"How much is it to get to Wedding?" I asked and gave him the address.

"About twelve euros. Are you getting in or what?"

I got in and the seat of the cab at that moment felt as cozy and warm as the bed I used to sleep in at my grandma's house when I was a child.

I enjoyed my ride, trying not to fall asleep, then the driver said something in German I couldn't understand.

"I don't speak German," I told him.

"Where are you from?" he asked me in English.

"Italy."

"Italy, uh… Berlusconi, bunga-bunga," he laughed.

"Yeah, pretty much," I said.

"I like Milan," he said, pointing his finger at a small pendant hanging from the rearview mirror.

"What's wrong with Hertha?" I asked him.

"Hertha? Uh? They are shit." He chuckled. "What's your team?" he asked.

"I don't have a team," I said.

"You're Italian and you don't watch football? You're strange, my friend," he said.

At least you don't see me jacking off in a cab under a bridge, I thought. "I do watch football, sometimes. It's just that I don't have a team. I like playing it."

"You play football?"

"I used to when I was a kid in my hometown. I was a goalie. You don't have to run a lot for that."

"You were good?"

"I was okay, I guess, apart from occasional lapses of concentration. My father said I daydreamed even during football."

"What?"

"Never mind," I said.

"You know who was a great goalie?" he asked.

"Who?" I asked, rubbing my eyes.

"Dida. Not very constant, but great player," he told me all excited. "Milan always had great defenders." And he went on, listing all the defenders that played for A.C. Milan from 1986 until recent years. He must have got to Jaap Stam, the Dutch giant, when things started to become hazy.

He stopped at a red light and kept talking. I must have been half asleep when I heard a sudden crash.

An arm holding a survival knife appeared from the shattered window and sliced the throat of the cab driver. He then tossed his body on the asphalt, sat on the driver's seat, and turned to me.

I recognized the man with the military jacket. "Your ride is over, Tony!" he said with a manic grin.

I woke up on the backseat of the cab. The driver's seat was empty and the door open. I checked his window, which was still intact. I felt for my phone and wallet. Still there and I had the twelve euros and forty cents. I got out of the cab and realized I was only two blocks away from home.

And the sun was rising.

"Why would they give this job to this daddy's boy?" Hector asked me during lunch break. "Why not Quique, who is the oldest and has done this shit for over three years? This kid is twenty-three, for Christ's sake."

Hector came from a small village next to Malaga, Spain. He had the typical Southern Spaniard look with very dark hair and eyes. Hector was an ambitious fella and always carried a notepad around the office. "Take note of everything they say," he kept saying, "one day it could save your life."

We both came from depressed towns in the south of Europe and that usually means something. We shared the same agenda and came to the big city for the same illusory need of self-determination.

"Does his age bother you?" I asked him, referring to Bernhard. My ears were still ringing from the concert.

"Doesn't it bother you?"

"A bit," I said. "He comes from a high-profile university. That must mean something."

"But still, he can't have more experience than Quique."

"Perhaps it's the hair."

"Quique is almost bald," Hector pointed out.

"Did you notice they all have that slicked back hair? Marcus and Lukas have it, same as the Re-Juvinator dudes. Bernhard has it too. Perhaps if we want to climb the ladder we should comb our hair that way."

"*Que cabron*," he laughed.

"How old are you?"

"Twenty-seven."

"Marcus too is younger than you," I said.

"I don't like this dude."

"Marcus?"

"I mean Bernhard. Marcus is a piece of shit, hands down."

"I don't mind Bernhard, despite his age and the Lord Fauntleroy look, he seems a decent guy," I said.

"Do you remember Raquel from the Spanish team?"

"Yes, she left two weeks ago."

"She should have left some months before."

"Uh?"

"Marcus didn't want to extend her internship when her first contract expired. That was over three months ago. She couldn't find anything else. Kind of a desperate situation. She had to sleep with him in exchange for a three months' extension," he said.

"Who told you?" I asked.

"She did," Hector said.

"Have you seen Juan today?" I asked him after a while. We were both done with our kebabs.

"I thought you knew he had to run to the hospital last night. You were at the concert with him, right?" Hector asked.

"Yeah, what happened?" I flinched.

"His girlfriend told me he was waiting for her on the platform at the U-Bahn station, when an inspector showed up and began harassing him to show his ticket. Juan didn't have one as he was only waiting for his girlfriend. He tried to explain that to the inspector but the man didn't speak English and grabbed Juan by the jacket. His girlfriend arrived just at that moment and saw Juan punching him in the face to escape the lock. Then they ran away but Juan didn't see a step and fell, breaking a rib. It seems his face is all roughed up too."

"Is he home now?" I asked.

"Yeah, he wrote me this morning. He was in bed playing *FIFA* and smoking pot. Have you heard what happened yesterday after the concert?"

"No," I said and wondered when the ringing would go away.

"They found five guys dead a few blocks away from the venue. The news was in the papers. All of them were stabbed. Apparently not exemplary citizens. One had just finished six months of probation for assaulting the Armenian owner of a convenience shop and breaking his cheekbones. Another was under investigation for the rape of a seventeen-year-old girl in a club."

I felt my heart jump. "Someone is going to have a toast today," I said.

"Yeah, the police are searching for a man with a military jacket, but I doubt one man could have carried that massacre out on his own."

"You don't say!"

The SEO team meetings took place every Thursday afternoon, and in those Bernhard mentored us about the whole SEO thing.

"SEO is a never-ending learning curve. Google constantly updates its algorithm, therefore we must catch up with it faster than our competitors," Bernhard said as we sat in the meeting room.

In those private universities they must teach you to speak in front of an audience. Bernhard was younger than most of us and I got the feeling that he couldn't care less about the job, but there was no doubt he could hold the stage. He was an intern like me, Hector, and Chris, with the difference that he was there to test his people management skills. The

SEO thing was only a pretext. Against a guy like Bernhard even Quique didn't have a chance. He had a running start on us and there wasn't much we could do about it, no matter how talented or ambitious we thought we were.

Those meetings revolved around Bernhard and Chris speaking. Bernhard was our team leader, while Chris liked to talk. We would make fun of Chris because of it.

That day Chris was hungover and fell asleep in the men's room. People searched for him for an hour until Joe, who went to take a piss, heard him snoring in the toilet stall and woke him up.

"We tried to call you," Quique reproached him.

"I lost my phone," Chris said.

"You're joking, right?"

That was the third time in two months someone had taken his phone. Every time the same story. After a night of revelry, he took the Ringbahn to get back home. Fell asleep in it. Circled the city one or two times. Woke up and realized someone had stolen his iPhone. Same thing happened with a cheaper smartphone he bought after the incident. At last he bought a forty euros phone with a normal keyboard. Chris thought they would spare him that one. He fell asleep in the Ring. They took that one too.

With the notepad in his hands, Hector would listen carefully to what Bernhard had to say, while Quique had put aside his initial frustration and became our quiet leader. Everyone, including Bernhard, would turn to him when things became hazy.

I asked few questions. Whether it was due to extreme caution or simple laziness, that I can't tell for sure.

There was a pleasant atmosphere in the team and, as delusional as it may sound, most of us felt as if we were evolving into something more than the cheap labor interns that we had been until then.

At least no one asked me again to assemble desks.

One day, while returning from lunch break, I found Bernhard sitting at the café's terrace next to the office building with a book and glancing at the Re-Juvinator girls who passed by. He had a yellowed pocket edition of Dostoevsky's *Notes from Underground* in his hands. No wonder some people found him pretentious.

"Hey Tony, I have found a cozy whisky bar around that corner," Bernhard said to me. He seemed excited about the discovery. "It's rather small but they serve brands from all over the world and I took a gulp before coming here." He looked at me as if he was expecting some manifestation of enthusiasm from my side. "Do you mind having a look?"

It was 20 to 2 pm; I figured twenty minutes was enough to go check it out, and technically it was my manager asking. "All right," I said.

He seemed to know one or two things about bourbons, scotch, wheat and all that. "Last year I had this one in Australia, it was a bar at a petrol station in the middle of nowhere, try it out."

The clerk took two short glasses and filled them. We both gulped them in one shot; it was sweeter than the commercial brands I was used to. As he slammed the glass on the counter, Bernhard yawped. "This one is on me," he said patting my shoulder. We left the bar.

"What is that you're smoking?" he asked.

I showed him a Marlboro Gold pack.

"Naaa," he exclaimed and took a blue pack I hadn't seen before from his pocket. "Try this", he said and handed it to me. "You'll thank me later.

"Say, Tony. How did you end up here?" He asked.

"You mean in the company or in Berlin?"

"I meant in the company but, what the hell, I want to know what brought you to this mad town."

"I met an Erasmus girl in Italy about a year ago," I said.

"Of course," he yawped again, "it has to be a woman!"

"And it seems underpaid internships are all this city has to offer for now," I said.

"What were you up to before?"

"I worked for a small travel agency and was about to start a master's degree," I said. "What about you?"

"Well, this thing I am doing is part of my bachelor's program," he said. "I need to complete a three-month apprenticeship and this company came along."

"Are you studying marketing?"

"Business administration," he said.

"But you have worked already in SEO, right?"

"Nope, this is my first experience in the field."

"Do you want to keep doing this after your studies?"

"Hell no," he said laughing. "I'd rather do something else. Write movie scripts and shit like that. I am very much into filmmaking," he said. "I'm considering applying to some film schools overseas after my bachelor's. What about you?"

"Me what?"

"What about your master's degree? You said you planned to start one before moving in here."

"Not sure I will do a master's, I'm kind of getting used to the employee life," I said.

"Dude, you joking, right?" His face had now turned serious. "You don't want to do link-building for the rest of your life. Do you?"

Marina found a job as a guide in a museum in the Ku'damm.

The situation at the catering job had become heavy on her. What made everything worse was the fact that Suzanna, the twenty-two year-old new wife of her boss, had been promoted to head hostess and started to act despotically toward her former peers, Marina included.

It's no surprise then that the new job came as a relief for her as she was finally able to quit the catering hell. The museum was dedicated to the history of Berlin, from its foundation in the twelfth century to the modern day.

On a Saturday she invited me to have a look around. She had spent two weeks memorizing the whole guided tour in German, Italian, and English and there was dedication in the way she showed me through the different sections. One could tell it suited her calling to become a teacher. I wondered if at one point in my life I will have the same dedication for what I do.

I particularly enjoyed the section about the early twentieth century which exhibited pictures of people such as Max Schmeling and Friedrich Wilhelm Murnau and objects belonging to them. Inside a glass case were Marlene Dietrich's travel suitcases. Three or four of them. Next to them, inside a smaller cabinet, was a yellowed letter addressed to her by Ernest Hemingway. *Dearest Kraut...* the greeting read.

At last she showed me the fallout shelter. The tour guides were over for the day. We were last.

"Do they have cameras in here?" I asked.

"A few," she said.

"Do you think they can see us where we stand?" I grabbed her by the waist.

"I'd rather not find out, at least not while I'm still on probation," she gave me a good kiss and we left.

That night as we were in bed I kept thinking of that old Hemingway letter and then, for some reason, of what Bernhard had said about doing SEO for the rest of my life, and that Ernest Hemingway and SEO are two things that couldn't possibly belong in the same thought, and that one day people will forget about Ernest Hemingway and how to write love letters, but they will know everything about SEO and how to set up a portable hotspot for the Internet. And so, that was it, one day school teachers will assign their students the reading of Jeff Bezos's memoir instead of *The Old Man and the Sea,* and in my own small way I was responsible for it.

Then we began hearing the neighbors upstairs. It was not the usual weird squeaking. They were having a fight. A big one.

A woman was hollering something in German.

"It's the black woman," Marina said, "the one we met in the staircase the other day."

Then a male voice screamed something else. He kept repeating the same sentence over and over but neither me nor Marina could understand it.

"That must be the guy who was with her," I said. He was a tacky looking skinny man I would also occasionally see smoking a cigarette in the courtyard. "They seemed cheerful the other day."

The woman would just respond with a "Jaaa… jaaa." It went on like a mantra. Sometimes she would alternate with "Neeein… neeein!"

"Wait," Marina said, "I think she said something like 'I dare you to touch me again.'"

We heard doors being slammed, furniture being hauled and furious footsteps that shook our ceiling.

"Should we go check?" Marina asked.

I didn't answer and kept staring at the ceiling, still thinking of Hemingway. Perhaps Bernhard was right. I had never set foot beyond European borders. At twenty-four one couldn't possibly think of settling down, let alone with a job like this. This should be only the first chapter of a bigger quest, then I should keep moving, seize the world. I had started my descent into an ordinary life. Wake up, go to work, go back to sleep, spend holidays at my parents' or at Marina's folks'. Have children, get a dog or a cat at one point, maybe both. Anything happening out of this sphere shouldn't concern me. Let alone a neighbor beating his girlfriend, wife or whatever that woman was to him.

"What's wrong?" Marina asked.

"That's the difference between you and me," I said. "You have Hemingway's love letter in the place you work, and because of me, boys and girls will have to read Jeff Bezos's biography at school."

"Who the fuck is Jeff Bezos? What are you talking about?"

"Forget it, let's go check," I said.

We went upstairs and knocked on their door. As we waited for something to happen, in my head I prayed that this guy didn't have one of those switchblades you see in movies. That wouldn't have surprised me, though. They didn't hear us and kept fighting and screaming. I banged on the door again.

"Should we call the police?" Marina whispered.

"Wait," I said, "it seems they stopped."

We waited at their door to make sure they had really stopped. Not a sound came from that apartment, it was as if they had suddenly frozen up or perhaps they ended up tearing each other apart and that would be the end of the squeaky sounds and the altercations. It was about 11 pm.

"Let's go to bed," Marina said.

As we walked to the staircase, a high-pitched scream came from the same apartment.

"WHAT'S WRONG WITH THESE PEOPLE?" I cried.

Then everything went silent again. It couldn't have come from the black woman, I thought. "Does anyone else live there?" I asked Marina.

"It must be the pale woman," Marina said.

"What pale woman?" I had never seen a *pale woman*.

"A few weeks ago some delivery guy left a parcel for us in their apartment. I had to knock and ring twice before I heard someone coming to the door. Then this woman opened, she seemed annoyed, *Biodeutsch* type, about our age. She gave me the parcel, not a word, and slammed the door in my face."

After about half an hour our lights were off and we heard another man in the building screaming. We couldn't understand anything since this one screamed in Turkish.

Was he scolding his wife? His daughter perhaps? Was he talking on the phone to his deaf aunt in Ankara? We heard no one complaining from the other apartments.

The voice kept growing louder and louder, as if in the entire district of Wedding it was the only thing one could hear. It went on for about forty minutes.

I got up and walked to the window. "Hey you," I called to the guy.

He kept screaming.

"*Hallo!*" I gave one or two more tries in a mixture of German and English.

Nothing, the thing went on.

"JESUS CHRIST SHUT UP!" I screamed in Italian.

That did it; let there be silence. I heard the noise of the neighbors slamming their windows. Not sure whether they opened them to look at what was going on, or they closed them, exasperated at the idea that an Italian had now joined the screamer's club. Marina laughed at my sudden outburst.

I returned to bed and tried to fall asleep.

*

Two men sat at a table in a crumbling bar with austere furniture. The tables were poorly lit and I couldn't see the faces of the figures sitting at them. They were done with their drinks and one of them waved at me.

I walked to them without realizing I was holding a tray. I reached the table.

"Bring me a whisky sour," one of them said.

I nodded.

"A beer," said the other one.

"What kind?" I asked.

"Doesn't matter," the man said.

Still, I couldn't see their faces, but I was able to glimpse some of their facial features. They both must have been about seventy years old.

There were other customers at the other end of the bar but I couldn't distinguish them either. They looked like shadows and stayed silent for most of the time but would occasionally whisper something to each other before going silent again. Their whispers sounded more like a buzzing.

I could feel some of them were looking at me and at the two men I was serving. Tiny, sparkling eyes watching us from darkness. Others didn't pay any attention to us.

The drinks – a whisky sour and a beer bottle – suddenly materialized on the tray I was still holding. There was a massive wooden counter at the center of the bar, but there was no bartender serving at it. Next to it four bar stools were vacant.

I walked back to the table with the drinks.

"Thanks," the whisky sour man said as he handed me a twenty German mark bill.

The other man took a hand rolled joint from his shirt pocket, placed it between his lips, and lit it with a match. The whisky sour man took a cigarette from an almost empty old Marlboro pack. The beer man began inhaling the smoke. One could tell it was good weed.

The shadows kept staring at us quietly from their corner and whispered.

"Want some?" The beer man asked the whisky sour man.

"No, thanks. I'd rather stick to my poison." The whisky sour man grinned as he held his glass. "That shit would kill my spirit."

"What about that shit?" The beer man pointed at the other man's glass.

"This keeps blood flowing into my veins. Say, how much do you smoke of that stuff?"

"Not much anymore. At least not as I used to." He took another hit. "I like to carry one with me wherever I go. Most of the time I don't touch it, sometimes even for a month. But today is an important day."

"It is," the whisky sour man said. "Isn't it?" he yelled, raising his glass in the direction of the sparkling eyes.

The shadows buzzed again, this time more loudly, before going silent.

"They have been waiting for quite some time," the whisky sour man said to his companion.

"Now they finally got their moment," said the beer man.

"How long has it been for you?" asked the whisky sour man.

"I've lost count. Maybe ten years. How about you?"

"Not sure either. I'd say more than that. Maybe twenty… twenty-five years… what difference does it make?"

"I am ready," said the beer man.

"Yeah, it's about time. I have seen enough of this."

"I can't deny I am still having fun. It's still quite a show out there."

"It depresses me."

"You used to say that even before."

"I did. But now it's beyond pathetic."

"Yeah…"

"Look at those devices they carry all the time. They don't even bother to check a piece of ass when there is one passing by. They are enslaved by those things."

"Have you seen those haircuts those muscular pricks wear? And how they dress! And you can't make fun of anything or they label you as an intolerant man. Everyone wants to control what you say. People get easily offended these days."

"We got in trouble during our days too…"

"True that. Yet it was different. There were people who craved a second voice back then. Not many, but there were. I say we were lucky we had people who listened to our ramblings."

"What if these were our days?" said the whisky sour man.

They stopped talking, just kept drinking and smoking.

Across the bar the buzzing intensified. All those shadows with their sparkling tiny eyes began bustling. Then they started moving towards us. They moved as a single mass of shadow and small, shiny dots glimmered and the buzzing became louder as they came closer.

In an instant they passed through me. For less than a second I found myself swamped by a black cloud and an unbearable, sharp buzzing noise. I then turned around and saw the shadows had now surrounded the two men sitting at the table.

The two companions didn't give any sign of concern. They just kept drinking and smoking. They had stopped talking.

The shadows moved closer and circled them. The two kept drinking and smoking undisturbed even as the shadows were now over them.

I couldn't see the two men anymore and I was still holding that tray.

The Re-Juvinator folks launched a new beauty product, which per se is something that shouldn't concern you or anyone else. Anyhow, for the promotion of the new product they made a music video. They didn't record a song but used a popular dance hit of that period and built the whole thing around lip syncing the lyrics and dancing around the office. And so for an entire day our office became a video recording studio in which all the Re-Juvinator people staged a choreography. We were instructed to just sit at our desks and work, not minding the turmoil and act as unaware background actors.

After about a dozen takes, in the late afternoon, they realized they couldn't do better and called it a day.

Later that week they held the video premiere party in a famous club in the district of Mitte. We received the invitation via email. Men were requested to wear a shirt, so I wore a wrinkled blue shirt that had been rotting at the bottom of my closet and went. Champagne glasses and appetizers were distributed throughout the place. I bumped into Joe who wore a white shirt.

"Nice shirt, Joe," I said.

"Piss off, queer," he said in embarrassment. He never attended any company event but for some reason he showed up that day.

Ashley joined us and clung to Joe's arm. She seemed already drunk.

"Don't get too close or you may upset him," I said to Ashley.

"Who? Joe? He is a big teddy bear," Ashley said and clutched his waist.

"Aren't you a big tough English teddy bear?" I said and patted Joe's shoulder, which felt as if I was patting a brick wall instead.

"That's it poof, I'm going to bust your ass," he said with a grin.

"I'll get something to drink," I said and walked away before he could actually bust my ass.

I walked to the bar and saw the Re-Juvinator folks with their slicked back hair and perfectly ironed shirts. Though we all wore a shirt, you could have easily guessed who worked at The Dancing Avocado and who at the Re-Juvinator. They took pride in showing their slim suit trousers and shiny moccasins.

They had invited a journalist who was interviewing their CEO in front of the cameraman, then the journalist turned her microphone to Anna who was wearing a long dark split dress with plenty of cleavage. Anna, with the microphone of the journalist raised at her face, saw me and smiled. I waved at her and reached Hector and Juan who were drinking bad red wine and looked as disoriented as I did. The other attendees drank sparkling wine.

I got some of that red wine which tasted like ashes dissolving in my mouth on that hot day of July. "Do they have beer in this place?" I asked the bartender.

"You need to go to the restaurant," the bartender said with a strong German accent.

We went to the restaurant and bumped into Bernhard. He looked happy to see me and dashed in my direction. "Tony, my brother, I have thought it through," he cried.

"What's up Bernie? What have you thought through?" I asked.

He grabbed my face as if he was about to kiss me on the lips. His breath smelled of whisky.

"What did you give him?" I asked Hector and Juan with Bernhard still clutching my face. The son of a bitch was strong. They didn't reply and kept watching the scene with an amused expression.

"Buddy, I have a great idea. We should leave, just the two of us," Bernhard said all excited.

"That sounds about right," I said. "Any place in mind? Perhaps the guys want to join too."

"No, you don't understand," he pressed harder on my face, "we should go on a trip. Leave Berlin, see the world. Suck out the marrow of life. This is our moment, we won't get another chance."

"Dude," I managed to free myself from his grip, "I think you are rushing here. What about your bachelor's degree? What about my girlfriend? And the job. Okay, let's face it, it's a shitty job, we all agree on that, but one has to put bread on the table," I said.

"Forget about that, your girlfriend will understand. The bachelor's, the job, it's all an illusion, my friend. We ought to leave, as soon as we can." He began hopping excitedly. Hector and Juan stood a few meters away, enjoying the scene.

"Alright," I said, "how are we gonna fund the whole thing? The flight tickets, the places to sleep?"

"We will sleep where we can. I have a spare sleeping bag back at my folks'. You can borrow it. You know what? It's yours."

"I thank you for that, but I barely make ends meet. I can't buy a ticket to Thailand or wherever it is."

"We will find work on the road. Use our hands like our ancestors did. And you know what, there is the account my father opened for my studies. He wouldn't mind if we borrow some of that money for the trip."

"You know what? Let's give it some more thought. It's this place. It makes us think unclearly. Let's get some beer," I proposed.

"You are a great guy, Tony." He smiled and hugged me.

82

"Yeah, you too, buddy," I said, patting him on his back.

At the terrace of the restaurant we found Adriana, Quique, and Chris having a contest to drink a half liter bottle of beer in one gulp. The three stood lifting the bottles and gulping from them with our other colleagues cheering, not minding the astonished glances of the other customers. It was a close bout.

Adriana and Quique appeared to have the edge over Chris who kept glancing at them, but it was clear he was losing ground. Then someone among the paying customers said something which made Chris sputter the liquid all over the floor.

"Okay, who said that?" He turned to the other customers rubbing his moist eyes and, as he began laughing, burped thunderously.

Adriana drained the bottle first and slammed it on a patio table. She gracefully rubbed her finger near her eyelashes and bowed before the others who cheered her. Soon Quique was done with his half liter, slammed it on the same patio table, and walked to Adriana with his arms spread, "what an incredible woman you are," he cried.

Ashley walked to Bernhard who stood next to me watching the contest, clung to his neck and together they walked away.

The open bar for the event attendees closed at midnight so we decided to make the best of it and began drinking and lighting cigarettes. After a while Quique got hold of a whisky bottle and began passing it around.

Soon we emptied the bottle and I walked to the men's room. There was no one in there.

I stood at the furthest urinal of the row doing my business when I heard someone walking in and taking the spot right next to mine. It's one of those unwritten rules. If you see a guy taking a piss at the end of the row, every individual with common sense would just take the spot at the other end.

Anyway, I decided to not let that distract me from concluding my business, but soon that strange feeling of being stared at got to me. I turned to my right and Marcus's frantic eyes were on me.

I got done as fast as I could and zipped my pants. "What's up Marcus?" I asked. He didn't reply but kept gazing at me with his mad, bloodshot eyes and manic expression. I assumed he was done too but he acted as if he had forgotten that he was still holding his dick in his hand.

"Do you see him?" he whispered.

"It's hard to miss it this close," I replied.

"You don't understand. He is here, he has found me," he said, still with his thing in his hand. I noticed he sweated copiously.

"See you, man," I said and walked to the sink.

Not a word from him; my boss was still glaring madly at me in the deserted bathroom of a well-known Berlin club with his thing in his hand and in an altered state. He finally zipped and began swinging all the toilet stalls open.

I washed my hands and looked at the mirror as Marcus bustled with the toilet stalls. I looked healthy, that was the face of a twenty-four-year-old, except I couldn't remember the last time I didn't have those circles under my eyes. Then in the mirror I saw this blond man standing right behind me and staring malevolently in my direction. He looked sick or something.

With a jolt I turned around and the sick man had disappeared. The men's room was empty except for Marcus now rolling about the floor.

I returned to the restaurant terrace where I found Hector visibly drunk. "Where the fuck have you been?"

"I went to take a piss," I said.

"*Que cabron*," he laughed and hugged me. "Juan is building a joint."

"There is a park nearby," I said.

"Too far. Let's find somewhere quiet."

We found Juan in a small hallway securing the rolling paper with his saliva. He had an amused expression and had unbuttoned his shirt at the height of his chest.

"Quique has found a place," he giggled and we followed him to a small back room where a dozen of our colleagues were sitting on stools or the floor. Quique sat in the middle of them with his leg crossed. He wore a straw hat and was playing an ukulele he had found in there. Next to him Chris was shaking two maracas while Ashley danced and the rest sang some Bob Marley song and drank. Bernhard was singing at the top of his lungs, sporting a woman's dress belt as a bandana. We joined them and Juan began passing the joint around and prepared another one while the others took their turns.

We camped in there, singing, smoking and drinking for about thirty minutes until Thomas, one of the Re-Juvinator folks, crashed our little party. He swung the door open and studied each of us – sweaty, drunk and high. Certainly in good spirits.

You could tell he was trying hard to find the guts to say what he wanted to say.

"Get the fuck out of here," he demanded at last and looked at us waiting for a reaction. We all stared back at him and at his still perfectly ironed white shirt which he had unbuttoned just enough to show a ludicrous golden chain that fell on his pale hairless chest.

After about five endless seconds of silence, the room burst into a mad laughter and Thomas stood there in embarrassment, not sure how to react.

"I will inform security if you don't leave now," he then threatened.

There was silence again.

"Let's go guys," I finally said and we all left, laughing at Thomas and patting his shoulder as we walked by.

The rumor of a group of dangerous drug addict squatters had quickly spread among the attendees of the party and as we returned to the main hall, all the eyes were on us. We kept drinking and enjoying our time like nothing happened. Joe walked to me and patted me on my cheek. "Well done, mate," he giggled as if he thought I was the instigator behind what had just happened.

Right at that moment they switched off the lights in the main hall and played the video for the new product launch on a giant white screen.

It starts with their CEO singing and dancing in the elevator, then the office door opens and we see two shirtless dudes carrying a desk on which sits an alluring girl wearing 80s fitness clothes and lip syncing the song. The camera moves to Anna, wearing similar 80s fitness clothes while singing and dancing. The most attentive viewers may notice Chris sitting at his desk in the background completely ignoring the instructions to act as an unaware background actor and staring open-mouthed at Anna. Again, this thing took at least eleven takes. Then it's Thomas's turn to perform in a rap solo. He was a pale German guy who loved hip hop, like many other pale German guys, and you could see he was having the time of his life rapping those verses. The video closes with all the Re-Juvinator folks reuniting in the backyard, looking lovingly and sending a kiss to the camera. For a few seconds in the video you could see me in the background, working at my desk. Unfortunately you can't anymore since the label controlling the song sued Re-Juvinator for copyright infringement and had the video removed from YouTube and the whole Internet.

When the lights were on again, the hall burst into an applause while I looked for something to drink.

"Do you think we will get into trouble?" Adriana asked me as we all left the club.

"I guess we will find out on Monday," I said.

*

Twenty-four missed calls. Jesus Christ. Twenty-four missed calls and nine text messages.

- *Why don't you pick up?*

- *I know you are with that whore.*

- *You're an asshole.*

- *I need to talk to you.*

- *I love you. Please, answer me.*

- *I am going to tell your sister. You leave me no choice.*

- *I just called your sister and told her you are with that whore.*

- *Where are you? Call me, please. I need to talk to you. It's important.*

- *Fuck you, Tony. I hate you and your damned whores.*

The guy who first came up with the idea of disabling the phone ringtone must have had his fair share of trouble. At least, I'm pretty sure it was a guy.

I looked outside. Clouds. Grayness. It was hot and sticky. I grabbed my laptop and sat on the bed. A squeaky student bed. Turned on the laptop. I tried not to wake her up.

She slept beautifully on her side. She was beautiful. Look at that jawline, I like a woman with a pronounced jawline. Look at those legs, those hips. What a marvelous creature. There was something broken about her I found irresistible. What was this thing I had with troubled souls? "Why can't you go out with the neighbors' daughter?" my parents used to reproach me when I was in high school. Her parents were both doctors. She was tall, had long legs and a pretty smile. She made me dull.

I opened Google. Jesus Christ, where do I start? I looked at my phone that lay on the desk. Well, I might as well give it a try.

She woke up. Stretched her arms and reached for my leg.

"What are you doing?" she asked with a charming, drowsy voice.

"Looking at something," I said.

"Two weeks we have sex and you already watch porn while I sleep. Am I that boring in bed?"

"There is always room for improvement."

She pinched me. It hurt. "Ouch," I went.

"You might as well stop playing the mysterious guy part. You have already hooked up with me," she said.

"Slept well?" I asked.

"Bla-bla-bla, what is that you're doing?"

"Just writing something," I said.

She sat on the bed and looked at the screen. "Is that a cover letter?"

"Yes," I said.

"What about the agency?"

"I will quit anyway, a few months won't make a difference."

"Well, you may want to justify the text. Also, add more line spacing otherwise no one will want to read it."

"Thanks," I said.

"Why are you writing it in English? Wait, I don't think *extensive* is spelled like that."

"You want to take a look?" I said.

"Sure, they teach us at school to write cover letters. It doesn't seem to be your case." She read the thing. "It's not bad. Wait, there is no recipient information."

I took the laptop from her and inserted the recipient information on the top left corner of the document.

Marina looked at it. "What does it mean?" She jumped from bed. "You must be kidding. You're kidding, right?"

"Why would I?" I was still sitting on the bed, working on the letter.

"I mean," she was trying to make sense of something, "you haven't even told your girlfriend about us. What about your master's? You told me you are supposed to start one in October," she said. She only had her panties and a tank top on. What a marvelous woman.

"I don't think I want to do it," I said. "I doubt I'll be able to go back to the student routine."

"You're not fucking with me, right?" she said.

"Listen," I said, "I'm sorry I freaked you out. But I think I have told you I want to try living abroad soon or later and I keep hearing how cool Berlin is. I'm turning twenty-four in a few months, it's a good age to give it a try. I'm just testing the waters here. Doesn't mean I will go all the way through."

"But…"

"I don't expect anything from you. I know you too are coming through a relationship. I'll get me a room somewhere. You don't have to see me if you don't want to."

"Are you sure you're not fucking with me?" Marina gave a shocked smile.

"Well last time we did was last night, remember? Am I that lousy in bed?"

"You're so fucked up," she cried and jumped back on the bed.

God knows for how long we stayed on that squeaky student bed.

Ashley, the American girl, didn't get her contract renewed by Marcus therefore had to buy a one-way flight ticket back to America as the company ceased to sponsor her working visa.

She was replaced by a guy – an I-am-a-Millennial-deal-with-it type of guy – who claimed that Heath Ledger was a better Joker than Jack Nicholson.

"Crap," I said one day during one of our many coffee breaks, even though I never was much of a coffee drinker.

"Dude, the guy won an Academy Award," Matt insisted.

"Sure he did."

"And you can't even compare the cinematography of the two flicks."

"*The Dark Knight* makes me dull," I said.

"You can't deny it's way more realistic though."

"It's based on a comic book, why does it have to be realistic?"

"Michael Keaton is so cheesy."

"Give me the cheesy Batman and the flashy costumes. WAIT… YOU SAYING CHRISTIAN BALE IS A BETTER BATMAN THAN MICHAEL KEATON?"

Matt arrived just on time to witness the downfall of our US market. They had been hit by a Google penalty, which is the worst thing that can happen to an e-commerce website. One of Google's employees caught Chris attempting to trick the algorithm by buying hundreds of back-links from a Bulgarian SEO agency. The agency home page header read something like *We skyrocket your Google rankings within two weeks.*

Chris managed to improve the rankings, but soon Google realized what had been going on for months, and removed our American website from its search engine. That meant that if every day there were a few thousands American citizens visiting the website through Google, after the penalty there was no trace of it. As a result, American people suddenly stopped downloading the app, and the company stopped making money from that market.

Lukas and Chris attempted to get in touch with Google for reconsideration with no luck. Chris was fired and the American market shut for good.

"He saw that coming," Hector said to me hinting at the fact that everyone in our team knew that Chris had been playing with fire for quite some time. That didn't stop many from being sad when he left. We all liked Chris.

We didn't see Marcus on those days as he stayed holed up in his office and I imagined that he was furious, therefore Lukas decided to handle the situation by himself to avoid throwing the team into more discomfort.

We would occasionally see Marcus dashing through the corridor to go speak to the team leaders. At times we saw him in the courtyard smoking a cigarette in a corner far away from the rest of us and brooding or walking back-and-forth. Sometimes he would do exactly that in the hallway. He struck as someone who struggled to enjoy quiet.

On one of those days I was getting on to work on my Monday morning tasks, mostly answering emails from bloggers. Forty-six unread emails in my inbox. I saw Marcus running past our row of desks and going toward Joe. Monday morning was always the most quiet moment of the entire week, while things became more lively after the weekly round-up meeting.

I heard Marcus as he approached Joe's desk.

"What is this?" Marcus had a paper in his hand that he shook at Joe's nose.

Joe was quiet, didn't seem concerned nor surprised to see his boss charging at him with that piece of paper and those frantic eyes that demanded an explanation. He seemed rather amused, although we all must have thought at that moment that flapping a paper or anything else at Joe was not a smart move. Marcus was twenty-five, Joe thirty.

"Those are our closed deals of last week," Joe said as if it were the most obvious thing to say.

That was not the answer Marcus expected. "Why do we have so many lost deals?" he yelled, waving the piece of paper closer to Joe's face.

Joe's expression darkened. "BECAUSE THOSE ARE LOST DEALS. Those prospects were not interested." As he stood up, Marcus took a step back.

"I have told you many times to label them as *on-hold* in these cases. You're not doing it right."

"You telling me how to do my job?" Joe roared.

They were equally tall, although at that moment Joe seemed to outsize Marcus. Marcus was tall but skinny while Joe was bulkier and looked like one thinks an English football hooligan should look like. He gave the idea of someone who didn't shy away from physical confrontation.

"I am the CEO here," Marcus screamed, "and you do as I say!"

Everyone stopped working. We all looked at them, waiting for anything to happen. No one at the near desks seemed afraid nor surprised. Some later said that they had seen it coming for months.

"You little cunt don't talk to me like this in front of my team," said Joe.

Marcus didn't see the insult coming. "What did you call me?" he yelled. There was madness in his eyes. There was always madness in his eyes, but this time it was different. A man who thrived on humiliating his subordinates, or whomever would come across him, could not accept being served the same dish.

He charged at Joe. That was not a reaction dictated by the need to restore his threatened honor in front of his employees. There was no pride in him, not in that particular situation, nor in his entire life. It was the instinctive reaction of a man who couldn't accept being contradicted or being denied anything.

Joe didn't seem to suffer the impact of Marcus charging at him, only after a few seconds he seemed annoyed, and with an effortless jolt he pushed his opponent away.

Marcus was thrown two meters away but immediately began to charge back, only this time Lukas grabbed him from behind. This made Marcus even madder. He tried to escape the lock but one of the Re-Juvinator folks, who in the meantime had been walking down the hallway with his headphones on, noticed what was going on and, with a dazed expression, stumblingly joined in support of Lukas.

"I am going to make your life miserable," Markus screamed and kept struggling his way out the lock like a trapped animal. "I don't want to see your face in here anymore."

Joe smirked. "Piss off, cunt!"

Lukas, with the help of the Re-Juvinator guy, succeeded in dragging Marcus away. Marcus eventually gave up and walked back to his office in fury.

We all returned to our Monday morning duties. Forty-six emails from fashion bloggers still waited for my reply. Nothing had changed.

95

In August Bernhard returned to Southern Germany to finish his studies. Some years later I had news that he had moved to Stockholm where he founded his own startup with another guy. They produced luxury bracelets, using only organic materials. They had a nice website with compelling imagery and video showing the hip streets of Stockholm with techno music in the background. The company lasted six months before shutting down. I like to believe Bernhard kept pursuing his ambition to become a screenwriter after that.

A few days later all employees were invited to Marcus's birthday party. The party was on a boat that would sail down the Spree. The appointment was at the river dock in Warschauer Strasse.

It was a 20-something-meter boat and everything was carefully prepared. A huge grill was being ignited on the deck. Three men were working at it. One was unpacking steaks, German sausages, and hamburgers. Another was unfolding their vegetarian variants, while the third man was arranging and slicing buns on a big tray. Next to the grill was a table filled with salads, toppings, and a variety of barbeque sauces. There was a third bar with a bartender serving beer and soft drinks and inside the boat was an even bigger bar which served hard liquors and cocktails. The drinks were free until midnight. No one cared to wait for the food before pouncing on them. Most of the people hurried to the beer counter while others ordered cocktails as appetizers.

We were not the only guests on the boat. Beside some of the Re-Juvinator folks, there was a group of five people sitting on the couches inside the boat. One of them had an orthopedic brace on his right leg which rested on a chair. They quietly drank their beer, not minding the maelstrom brought by us. At first I thought they were friends of Marcus, but they turned out to be other paying guests.

Almost everyone showed up, except Joe and his team. It was rumored that they decided to boycott the event. I liked the idea of boycotting our boss's birthday party but Hector convinced me otherwise. "The fuck do you care? You got free booze, food and we are going to have a good time. Come on *cabron*!"

I found Juan and Hector leaning against the pushpit at the stern of the boat. They were talking while Juan was intent on building a joint. Quique, Adriana, and Marta from the Spanish team stood a few meters away, each of them had a drink in their hands.

"Look who is here," Marta shouted.

"They said you were thinking of ditching us," Adriana said.

"Do you believe everything Hector says?" I said.

"Adri, you shouldn't trust an Andalusian," Juan said.

"*Coño* Juan," Hector said. "What made you change your mind, *cabron*?" he asked me.

"That thing you said about free booze."

"Are you sure it is not because you ran out of weed at home?" Quique sneered.

"You came just to see Anna sunbathing on the deck," Marta said to Quique.

"The woman is right, has anyone seen her?" Quique shouted.

"I have," Juan said and handed me the joint, I took one hit and passed it around.

"Is it true Re-Juvinator is going through some rough times?" Hector asked.

"They might shut business soon," Quique said with a saddened expression.

"Who told you?" Hector asked.

"They asked me for a marketing consultation. They have gone almost one month without a sale. The video was just a last, desperate attempt to get back on track."

"He is a big shot now," said Juan referring to Quique.

"What are we going to do without Anna in the office?" Quique protested.

"Oh, look at you!" Quique said to a blond girl who walked by. She worked for the German market. They began talking before disappearing together.

"And off he goes," Hector said. "Let's get something to drink."

"*Vamos*," Marta said.

"Tony," Adriana grabbed my arm as I began following the others, "isn't your internship ending soon?" She was still jovial in her own way but something had begun wearing her out. There was a hollowness in her eyes I only then noticed.

"In two weeks," I answered.

"Have you talked to them?"

"Not a word from them yet."

"But you would like to stay, right?"

"I guess," I said.

"Tony, do you remember what happened to Monica?"

"I do."

"How do you manage to be so calm? I would be freaking out if I were you."

As Adriana and I walked to the deck, we bumped into Thomas from

Re-Juvinator. Marcus had invited him too for some reason.

He was drinking alone, leaning against the pushpit. In normal circumstances Thomas avoided small-talk like the plague, but when he got drunk he seemed to regress into a hollow half-wit.

"Italiano," he shouted. "Berlusconi, mafia, bunga-bunga," and laughed proudly as if he were the first to come up with such scoffing.

"Kiss my ass," Adriana said to him.

"Anytime, *Schatzi*. Hey mafia boy," he said to me, "how many did you whack today?"

"Hey Tommy," he didn't like being called that, "let's invade Poland. You and me."

"What?"

"Sure, we can handle them. The moment they see you knocking at their door they will pee their pants."

"Dude, I'm half Polish."

"Oh, sorry, didn't know that," I said. "Hey Tommy."

"What now?"

"You're sunburning, buddy," I said.

The sun had hit hard on his ghost-like skin during the sailing. He wore a tank top. White guys shouldn't be allowed to wear tank tops in the first place. He also wore that hideous golden cross. Anyhow, Thomas seemed unaware of the new pigmentation of his skin that now resembled that of a crab. Thomas, the Giant Crab of the Spree. His skin must have itched like hell, and he began wandering around the deck on his own with his beer and cigarette, trying to act cool about it.

Despite all our differences, we were having a good time and very few seemed to be there with the least intention to celebrate Marcus.

Marcus looked happy. He was perhaps the only person I had ever seen who looked more frightful when he was happy than when he was angry. He still had that frantic look in his eyes which was now combined with a crooked grin. Even more terrifying was the fact that he greeted anyone whom he saw showing at his party, including the interns to whom he had never spoken.

I was dealt with a "Hi, thanks for coming!"

Despite sporadic attempts to interact with his employees, for most of the time Marcus hung with Lukas, Anna, and the other Re-Juvinator people. He did his best to show he was having a good time.

Before 10 pm we had already sailed through the Kreuzberg-Friedrichshain District with no particular accidents and were entering Mitte. Someone had thrown up into the river and Quique had been yelled at by the boat staff as they caught him having sex with the German girl in the bathroom. Marcus didn't drink much but would occasionally move away from the rest, together with one or two guys from Re-Juvinator, and when he returned his eyes looked even more frantic.

The other five guests of the ship were still on their couches. They kept drinking and chatting peacefully. Lukas, Adriana, Quique, Anna, and I were sitting at a table next to theirs as Marcus walked in. He wanted to sit with us but there were no spots left.

Lukas offered to squeeze across so that Marcus would fit, while Marcus was now staring at the guy with the orthopedic brace on his leg. He looked about the room until he directed his glance at a small crate used to store empty beer bottles. He ran toward it, grabbed it, and walked toward the plastered guy, holding the crate.

"How about you lean your leg on this, so I can use that chair?" He asked the guy.

The plastered man looked at him with a mix of disbelief and amusement for the unusual request. "That is too small," he said smiling at him. "I need to keep it high."

Marcus looked about again until he found a new crate. "You can put that crate on top of this one. Would that work?"

"Dude, I broke my leg two weeks ago. I have to rest it on a soft surface." The plastered man was not smiling anymore, he seemed rather embarrassed. His friends glared at Marcus. "Why don't you just sit on the armrest of that couch?" one of them suggested.

"Why don't you shut the fuck up?" Marcus responded to that suggestion and turned to the man with the broken leg. "Dude, I'm going to sit. You can use the fucking crates or rest your leg on your friend's lap."

I saw Anna stand up and hurry out to the deck.

"Forget it," the man with the broken leg replied to Marcus and sipped his beer trying to act as calm as he could.

With a jolt Marcus grabbed the chair from under his leg. The guy let out a scream as the leg hit the floor. One of his friends stood up and charged at Marcus. He had him by the collar of his shirt. Quique and Lukas stepped in, trying to separate the two. The friend of the plastered man gripped Marcus firmly. The three other friends, who until that moment seemed to be interested only in enjoying their beer, backed him up. Marcus didn't show any sign of fright at the guy gripping him. He had the expression of someone who had just awoken and didn't quite understand what was going on. Lukas and Quique, with the help of the plastered man's friends, succeeded in separating them. The guy loosened his grip reluctantly, while Marcus was still standing in front of him, not giving any sign he wanted to retreat or resume the dispute. He looked to be in a trance-like state. The plastered man had stopped screaming and was still watching the scene and holding his leg with both hands.

Then Marcus went out on the deck, lit a cigarette, and began looking for Anna.

Not much happened for the rest of the sailing. The bar had stopped giving free drinks and the demeanor of the passengers was slowly blowing over.

I walked to the stern and lit a cigarette. I felt a warm emptiness filling me. The boat was illuminated by the starry midsummer night and from there the people on the river's bank looked like tiny shadows drinking, walking their dogs, and riding their bikes.

I looked at the others leaning on the pushpit or sitting wherever they could, chatting, smoking, and sipping the last warm beer they were able to get for free. Lost souls doomed to cut through the waters on a ghost ship.

We split as the boat docked. People headed home or somewhere else.

"How about a beer for the way?" Hector proposed.

"*Vale*," said Quique as we headed for a *Spätkauf* across the dock.

It was a warm and starry night in August but a brisk breeze was rising.

*

"We want to offer you a contract as SEO lead for the Italian market," Lukas said to me a few days before the end of my six months internship. He seemed happy to offer me the job.

My salary was raised to 1,600 euros, a bit over 1,200 after tax. The early days spent assembling IKEA desks for 400 euros a month seemed long gone.

My tasks did not change, however. Not a bit. The bloggers kept sucking a considerable part of my working life and the most frightful part of it was that I was becoming good at dealing with them.

Joe left soon after. He was not fired; he had found another job somewhere else.

"If you want to make something out of your life, do the same," Joe told me on the day he left with his usual brotherly affection. "Take care, fag!"

He had a point, I thought. Who would want to work for a psycho and deal with those bloggers on a daily basis for an indefinite amount of time?

But hey, I was not an intern anymore!

Part II

Next thing I knew I had spent three years at The Dancing Avocado. One would be surprised how the eight hours' working routine alters one's sense of time.

You wake up, have breakfast, take a shit, shower and brush your teeth, take public transport, spend eight hours of your day sitting on a chair staring at pictures of clueless young women pulling a duckface and wondering when the next pandemic is going to wipe us out, perhaps have one of two beers with your work pals, go back home on public transport, have dinner with your girlfriend and talk about your day or something entirely different, sit on the couch, watch *Breaking Bad* or *The Twilight Zone*, roll a joint, smoke it, maybe make love if the two of you are not too drained by the day, or even if you are that upset that you need sex to erase from your mind the degradations you have endured during the day, goodnight kiss and fall asleep.

And of course there are the unreasonably high-priced hip restaurants, the trips, the things you buy on the Internet that make you think you fit in as long as you have enough money in your bank account and that you are too good for your job and perhaps you should find something better for you, something worth-committing to it. But then your bank account says you have only twenty-one euros and fourteen cents left and there is still one week to pay day and so, after all, you realize you are bound to your job no matter what kind of a miserable empty shell of a person it has turned you into. And when your employer refills your bank account at the end of the month you start over again.

And things change in three years and, perhaps, you change too.

People left the company and others arrived to replace them. Those who stayed did their best to climb the company hierarchy, like Adriana who had become Head of Customer Relation Management, which means that she was responsible for the content that we sent out via newsletter to our customers, and as a result she had Marcus constantly by her neck, so perhaps, despite the promotion, her life had become more miserable than mine. Others like Hector found fortune outside the company, as my pal was offered a managerial position at the London headquarter of eDeals, the American multinational e-commerce corporation.

The changes didn't just apply to The Dancing Avocado, though. Soon after Lukas offered me the contract, Re-Juvinator shut down business and from one day to the next in the office there was no trace of Anna and the whole glossy bunch.

*

I asked Quique for a raise. He seemed surprised, not for the fact that I asked for a pay raise, but for the fact that I asked him directly. "I will mention that to Lukas during our next meeting," he said.

Lukas invited me to follow him into his office a few days later. As I entered the room, Marcus was there. He stood in a corner, brooding, unaware of my presence.

"So, Tony," Lukas said, "Quique told me about your request."

"That's correct," I said. "Since we are here, this could be a good opportunity to discuss my future in this company."

He smiled. "Absolutely," he said. "You see, Tony, we both are businessmen and I feel that I can speak frankly with you."

"Go ahead," I said. I'm still not sure how I felt about him referring to me as a businessman.

"As you are aware, we are going through some big structural changes in this company. We have been through a challenging quarter and we are currently in a phase in which we need to consider different aspects."

"I understand," I said, trying to get past the businessman thing.

"We value you as a professional and as a person. Everyone in this company is fond of you, and we want you to be part of our future."

"I appreciate that," I said. "So, concerning my request, when will you be able to give me an answer?"

"I would say in two weeks."

"That works for me. I too want to be honest with you," I said.

"Please, go ahead," he said with his usual politeness.

"I have been contacted by recruiters lately. And I want you to be prepared in case I might find a good fit for me." I didn't brag about it. It was true that I had received some messages on LinkedIn from recruiters. The thing is that I never took them too seriously and replied only to a few. I had also sent some applications to companies but after the first rejections, I quickly got over it. So, in the end, I said that to put pressure on him, hoping that he would agree to give me the raise.

"Thanks for being honest," he said. "You should do what is best for you and your ambitions."

That in my head sounded like, *Finally he is getting the hell out of here*.

We shook hands and I returned to my desk.

In the meantime Marcus had found love. According to the office gossipers, it was true love and a few weeks after they began seeing each other, they even decided to move in together. So from one day to the next this woman began coming to the office with him.

She was the opulent type, with lips that seemed a bit out of proportion, and every day would show up at work with shiny design garments and sumptuous hats that clashed with the surrounding environment, especially now that the Re-Juvinator folks were gone. And with the two of them came this white teacup poodle.

The poor beast was scared to death by anyone in the company and would follow his owner everywhere she went or would simply snuggle up in a corner in Marcus and Lukas's office. He – Coco was his name – acted somewhat afraid of Marcus too, something which most people would find understandable, but seemed to tolerate him more than the rest of us.

"Look at this cutie," exclaimed our Italian colleague Lorenzo one day when he noticed the disoriented dog scampering in the hallway, looking for his owner.

I saw Lorenzo stretch his arm to pet him, then let out a high-pitched scream. "OH JESUS," he shouted. "OH SHIT," and he jumped up from his chair.

The poodle had interpreted his gesture as hostile and began barking furiously at him. Lorenzo was crouched on his chair, staring terrified at the minuscule pet.

"Where is the dog?" Marcus shouted as he walked out of his office.

Coco, who in the meantime had retreated to find shelter, found himself between the stern look of his new master and the plants that enclosed the lobby.

"Come here," Marcus shouted at the dog.

The thing looked at him and retreated below one of the plants. He then stared at Marcus with those tiny black eyes from there.

Marcus kept shouting at him to make him follow him to his room. The dog moved a few steps toward him hesitantly and, when he was within reach, Marcus grabbed him and ran to the room with the dog in his hands.

To give Viktoria some credit – that was our new first lady's name – she seemed to get the best side of Marcus. According to the same office gossipers, he had quit his habits involving drug consumption and even smoking. As a result, we wouldn't see him anymore roaming nervously around the office like he used to and he had even gained some weight. He showed a healthier look and those cheekbones that had become part of his tyrant-like face had become less protuberant.

Even more shockingly, he had become by some degree even less abominable to us. He was still the same money-driven piece of shit who thrived in making his employees' lives miserable, but perhaps a bit less than before. So, in the end, everyone in the office welcomed Viktoria with due enthusiasm.

What better time to ask for a pay-raise now that this man had found true love?

"I think I might leave," I said that day to Adriana during cigarette break.

"You said that last month," she replied. "How many applications have you sent since then?"

"None," I said.

She laughed. "Didn't you want to ask for a pay raise?"

"I did,"

"And?"

"I doubt it is going to happen," I said. "Lukas said they will get back to me with an answer in two weeks."

"If I were you, I would really start looking around," she said.

"Am I that hopeless?" I asked, but I knew she had a point.

"I had lunch with Quique the other day and for some reason the conversation moved to you."

"What did he say?"

"He said you do your job well and are the most experienced in the team, but you do just what you are asked to and not much more. He sees you don't care too much at the end of the day," she said.

"Uh?"

"You act as if everything that happens here doesn't affect you more than it should. I am not saying it is bad, it's part of your character and the people here love you because of this, but I doubt this will help you with Lukas and Marcus to get a raise," she said.

"How about Marcus? Is he treating you well?"

"Every time I have a meeting with him is like watching an *American Horror Story* episode," she said. "I would rather go back to serving tables for five euros an hour than do it one more time."

Those three years had altered her appearance and her mind too, like the rest of us, after all. Her expression had hardened. She was still one of the most beautiful women in the office, but her face had hollowed and her hair had lost its shine. She would spend nine to ten hours in the office every day, then end up in some club drinking, popping pills, hooking up with some guy she had met on Tinder. She always told me about them. She told me she was trying to cut down on the drinking. And the pills. I told her she should have started by cutting down the ten hours first.

"How is your job-hunting proceeding?" I asked her.

"I have an interview tomorrow with Cuckoo, I told you about that. The first round went well, at least I passed it, but this is going to be the end of my ride. The interview is with the CMO."

"You will kill it," I said.

And she did, she got the job and, within a few weeks, Adri was gone.

*

"I'm late," Marina said as I got home.

"I am late," I said. "I had a beer with the guys."

"I'm worried since I have given up the pill." She kept biting her nails.

"What's to worry about? We have been careful, besides you're always late."

"We haven't been careful in the last weeks."

"That would be like fate giving us the middle finger for that one time we crossed the line."

"It was not only that time. We deserve it. We are terrible people."

"Not more than the rest."

"Can you be serious for once?"

"I can't. Otherwise I will be reacting just like you. This couple needs someone to break up the tension."

"You saying I might have been knocked up by my comedy sidekick? How pathetic is that?"

"All right, if we hurry we might make it to the drug store before it closes," I said.

We made it to the drug store. It was four minutes to 9 pm. Marina took from the shelf a pack of two pregnancy tests.

"Why did you take two?" I asked as we waited at the cash register.

"They ran out of one-piece packs."

"I told you we are not worse than the rest."

We left the store with our pregnancy tests.

As we waited at the traffic light, a woman across the street began running in our direction, not minding the red light. Just before reaching the sidewalk, she began hopping awkwardly on one leg then on the other. Right when she made it to the sidewalk, with a jolt she dropped her baggy pants, crouched down, and peed right in front of the two of us.

"And one day our child will call this home," I said.

The day after, Marina got up early and ran to the bathroom. I can't tell how long she stayed in there but to me it felt like an eternity. Not a sound came from the bathroom and I thought I must have done or said something wrong and she was doing it on purpose to get back at me. Or perhaps she was crying in shock. *Should I go check on her? Why is she taking so long, for Christ's sake?* I promised myself that would be the last time I let down the guard.

Then I heard the flush. She came out of the bathroom and walked back to the bedroom. I felt my heartbeat.

"Negative," she said.

She climbed back on the bed and nestled against me.

"Let's be careful from now on," she said.

"I agree."

"What if it were positive?"

"That would be your call at the end of the day."

"I just want to know what your reaction would be," she insisted.

"We are lucky it's not," I said. "Before you said negative, right?"

She smiled. "Do you think I would joke about this?"

"Well, you made me paranoid already."

"But what if it were?"

"Why are you doing this?"

"I just want to know."

"Last thing we need now is a child. We don't have enough money, this apartment is not good for a child, and chances are I will leave The Dancing Avocado soon."

"Didn't you ask for a raise?"

"I did. It's very unlikely I will get it."

"Does it mean you have to leave?"

"It's about pride."

"Since when are you all about pride?"

"If they see you have no ambition, they take you for granted," I said.

Turned out I too can be right sometimes.

*

The two weeks went by.

"So, did you have a chance to speak to Marcus?" I asked Quique in the office kitchen while he was pouring filtered coffee.

He hesitated. "I did."

"Cool, how did it go?"

"I mentioned that to him during our last meeting, we discussed many topics, as always."

"Do you know if Lukas has mentioned it to him in the last two weeks?"

"I can't tell, but I asked him about your pay rise,"

"What did he say?"

"He said he doesn't have the time to think about it." I felt the disappointment in his words.

"It's all right," I said, patting his shoulder as if he was the one needing solace.

The time to freshen up my resume had come.

I worked on it during work time. One never realizes how time consuming it is to list all your career achievements in a way that convinces the recruiter who is going to read them that you're not a total loser. Even when the achievements are rather meager, to say the least. But still, for the job market, I was not a clueless intern anymore, but a sought-after young professional destined to make the fortune of any ambitious tech company in Berlin.

I began sending applications every day. One day I had sent a whopping twenty-one applications. Out of which seven replied. At first I aimed high. Head of SEO, Head of Content Marketing, even Italian Country Manager for a big multinational corporation.

A few of them even granted me an interview, only to startle when they realized I had no idea of what I was doing there.

It's all about managing your expectations, they say.

*

I was sitting in this room. It was a very bleak room with no furniture in it, except for some chairs and a small table in a corner with rusty legs. Other people were sitting on those chairs. A bald guy of about my age with jeans cuffed at his ankles and a t-shirt that read *Ok, but first coffee,* was sitting in front of me. He had his headphones on, a Starbucks tumbler in one hand and his smartphone in the other. He noticed me staring at him and gave me an annoyed gaze. A few chairs away, sat this woman. About my age too, Asian roots. She wore an elegant black, long dress that fell just above her leather wedge heels and a black leather jacket. She had placed her black leather briefcase on a chair next to hers and was reading something on an e-reader.

A woman pushed a metallic door open. "Antönio La Mattina, you may follow me."

I followed her.

"Take a seat, Antönio."

"It's Antonio," I said.

"What?"

"Antonio," I said, "my name is pronounced *Antonio.*"

"What did I say?" She raised his eyes from a file she had been reading and began studying me. It was a voluminous pile of paper. She placed it on the desk and sighed. She took off her reading lenses. Placed them on the desk, near the file. She had a mullet and the thickest neck I had ever seen. I couldn't stop staring at that neck.

"Age?" She asked.

"Twenty-seven," I said and she double-checked something on the file.

"Height."

"1,83," I think. She checked on the file again and sighed.

"Weight.

"It ranges," I said.

"What do you mean?" She sighed again. That neck seemed to grow thicker by the minutes.

"Between 75 and 80," I said, "not sure about now."

She took a look at my figure and scribbled something on the file. The file was as thick as her neck. I kept moving my gaze between the file and the neck. The rest of her and that room was simply too much to handle without going mad.

"Size of shoes?"

"45."

She looked at my shoes. "Are those the sneakers, model Converse All Star, color black, you purchased on the 12th of October 2014?"

"That's correct," I said.

She flipped a page, studied it carefully and glared at me in disgust.

"Do you have a smartphone?" she asked.

"Yeah, bought it last year."

"Good," she crossed something on the new page.

"What brand?"

"Lenovo. It's Chinese, I think."

"You have a Facebook account?"

"Yeah."

"Instagram?"

"No.

"Twitter?"

"No," I said.

She glared at me again.

"In the last year you have watched at least one episode of *Breaking Bad, The Sopranos, Monty Python's Flying Circus, Curb Your Enthusiasm* and *The Twilight Zone*. Is that correct?" she asked.

"That is correct," I said.

"What's wrong with *True Detective*?"

"I have given it a try," I said. "Matthew McConaughey makes me dull."

"But I don't find a Netflix subscription in here." She raised her eyes again from the file and studied me.

"That's because I don't have one," I said.

She looked at me worriedly and flipped a page again.

"Do you listen to techno?"

"No."

"Hip hop."

"Nope."

"What's this thing you have for Captain Beefheart and His Magic Band?" She asked.

"What's wrong with Captain Beefheart and His Magic Band?" I replied.

"I ask the questions," she grumbled. "Do you have a Spotify account?"

"I do," I said.

She looked relieved.

"Are you a vegetarian?"

"No."

"Vegan?"

"Nope."

"Are you celiac?"

"No."

"Lactose intolerant."

I said no. She flipped the page again.

"Religious views?"

"I don't have any," I said.

"Ass or breasts?" she asked.

"What?"

"Are you gay, bisexual, pansexual or considering undergoing a sex change operation in the near future?"

I said no to all of those.

"Do you like a woman with big breasts or you would consider yourself as an ass-man?"

"I would say an ass-man."

"Are you into one of the following porn genres?" And she went on listing different genres of porn, one or two of which I had never heard of.

"No," I said.

"You're not on Tinder," she pointed out.

"How is that a problem?" I said.

"I ask the questions," she roared and her neck bulged. "Do you own a Tinder account?"

"No," I said.

"How come?"

"I live with my girlfriend."

"Is she on Tinder?" she asked.

"Not that I know of," I said. "It's hard for me to find out without owning an account myself."

"Are you being a smart-ass?" she roared again and the neck had now assumed monstrous proportions.

"Of course not," I said.

She studied me in silence for some minutes, before turning to the file. She began scribbling something on it, then picked up the receiver of a phone that lay on the desk and waited until someone picked up on the other end. "Yes… I'm done with the sample number 22,054,355," she told her interlocutor.

She hung up and closed the file. Someone opened the door and walked in. He was an everyman wearing an overused brown suit. He had a worried expression.

They began whispering to each other at the other end of the desk, while the woman with the mullet and the bullneck stared at me.

The man with the worried expression walked over to me. "You're not ready," he said with his worried face and beckoned me to follow him.

"Ready for what?" I asked.

He didn't answer and pushed me through a series of metallic doors.

"What should I be ready for?" I asked him again. Then, as we walked through one of those bleak corridors, I heard it.

It was a maddening, shrill metallic roar that made the entire place shake. It lay deep at the bottom of that bleak place calling for me. Calling for all of us.

The worried man swung one last metallic door and pushed me out onto the streets.

I was out, at least for now. I was still in Berlin, dark and harsh, and I wondered if I was actually *out*.

An old homeless man walked by. He saw me and muttered something in his *Berliner Schnauze.*

"What?" I said.

He burped right in my face – *that must be what death smells like*, I thought – and walked away.

Berlin is like a painting someone got tired of finishing.

*

It took me three months. Dumboo, the homestay marketplace backed up by Platypusnetic, sought an SEO Manager for their Italian market. It was not the first time I showed my interest in working for them as, in fact, I had already applied twice to them.

This time they invited me to have an interview in their office with their Head of SEO. He was a chunky guy in his early thirties from Spain. His hair was streaked with grey and he had a friendly face. I was expecting some German guy with stern eyes and that typical slicked back hairstyle. Things were finally turning in my favor, I thought.

He had a broad smile, and I found it difficult not to smile back at him. Santi began introducing himself. He spoke with a strong Spanish accent and explained to me he came from a town near Valencia and he had started working at Dumboo only one month earlier.

Months of job interviews must leave you with something, and I realized I was well prepared for this one. I asked the right questions and gave him the right answers. We talked about SEO and he briefed me about the company and what they looked for to fill the position.

"What strikes me about your application is the record of link-building partnerships you have developed." He seemed impressed, which made me think that the past three years must have served some purpose.

The conversation then turned into a chat about our respective hometowns and I even exhibited some Spanish words I had learnt with the guys at The Dancing Avocado. He seemed pleased about that too.

As I left, he walked me back to the door and shook my hand, giving me his broad smile. "Good luck, Tony" he said.

They sent me an email that same afternoon in which one of their recruiters invited me for the next round, the following week.

I went. The first interview was with the same recruiter, Katharina was her name.

"Why do you want to leave your current company?" She asked as we sat in a small room.

"I want to embark on a more ambitious project," I replied.

"What do you expect to find here?"

"The chance to gain valuable skills and to work in the travel industry, which is one of my greatest interests."

"Where do you see yourself in five years?"

"Running my own business," I replied.

"What kind?" she asked.

"Digital publishing," I said, and I felt it gave her a good impression of me as someone who wants to make a career in the field.

"What do you do in your spare time?"

"I listen to music and travel," I said. "Sometimes simultaneously."

"If you were a famous actor, who would you like to be?"

"John Belushi."

"Isn't he the guy in *According to Jim*? I loved that show," she said.

"That's his younger brother. John is dead."

She paused before moving to the next question. "How many windows are in Berlin?"

"Eighteen million," I replied.

"How did you come up with that number?" she asked.

"Seems like a good number to me."

"If you were a shoe, what shoe would you be?"

"A flipflop."

After Katharina was done with her questions, she asked me to wait on my seat. "Do you need a glass of water?" she asked before walking off.

She returned with another woman who sat next to her. "Please, meet Alessandra," she said. "She is in charge of SEO for the Italian market. You would work closely with her."

"Good to meet you," I said.

"Hi," Alessandra replied.

"Do you have some questions for Tony?" Katharina asked Alessandra.

"Yes…" she said. She didn't make much of an effort to hide her irritation toward the situation. "Can you tell me a bit about yourself?"

I repeated what I had already told Katharina, who looked annoyed, not by me but by Alessandra and kept glaring at her.

Alessandra began asking more technical questions related to SEO. I answered each of them with little effort. I felt it didn't please her. She stared at me with contempt behind a thick layer of make-up. She was the gothic type, with black, straight hair dyed at the ends and black, polished fingernails. Perhaps the attitude was part of the character, I thought. Maybe, after you have broken the ice, she becomes the best colleague one could dream of.

Then she began questioning some of my answers. "I believe that social media has an impact on SEO."

There you go, I thought, here she makes one last attempt to sabotage my hiring and, for some reason, Lucia and Monica popped into my mind. Why in every new job must there be some passive aggressive fellow countrywoman who hates me because she is convinced I am there just to steal her job and make her life miserable? Aren't we supposed to be supportive to each other in a foreign land?

"Actually Google stated that social media isn't a direct cause of good rankings. On the other hand, it could have a positive impact by driving traffic. Therefore the effect is indirect," I said. In three years I had learnt one or two things and that didn't please her one bit.

I got the job. The following day I informed Lukas who seemed surprised at the news that such a big company would offer me a job. He agreed on granting me a two weeks' notice period rather than the full month according to the contract. Lukas was a good man. I informed the others. I was relieved, yet I was leaving behind some fine people.

Marina and I decided to celebrate. We had dinner at a sushi place in Mitte and spent the weekend between the bed and the couch. On Sunday morning, Marina dragged me out of bed and we took a stroll at a nearby park. She enjoyed nature and taking long walks surrounded by trees and picnics on sunny days. She was still half-German, after all. Later that day we purchased a last minute flight to Southern Spain.

*

We flew on a Thursday. Our flight departed at 7.30 am from the Schönefeld Airport and we made it just on time. We landed and it was hot. It was hot when we waited at the baggage claim and it got hotter when we went to pick up the car at the rental. *What better occasion to test my Spanish*, I thought.

The car rental clerk dumped some ridiculously priced insurance on me.

"But I bought the full CASCO coverage when I booked," I said to him. I had already switched to English after realizing the guy was up for promotion that day.

"That only covers you with the third party company you have booked through," he said. He spoke with a ceremonious tone, as if he was trying to convince me that I would have made a terrible mistake had I declined that offer. Not only for my wellbeing. I felt that the destiny of my beloved ones, of the folks back in my home town in Italy, even of the *Spätkauf* clerk that sold me cigarettes, depended on whether I would have bought that damned insurance that day. He wore a short sleeved white shirt, and he was fat and despite that, not a drop of sweat fell from his temple as he had one of those portable desk fans pointed straight at his face.

"What does it even mean?" I asked. "What did I purchase that other insurance for then?"

"All right, I can give you a discount only for today. Fifty instead of one hundred," he said. As if next time I will fly to that place, I will rent a car from the same agency and ask to be served by that fat dude who was such a blast to have a chat with.

I gave him the fifty and took the car. It was a nice car, German manufacturer, with the Bluetooth system that plays the music you have in your phone.

"Can't we listen to something more in the mood?" Marina protested.

"What's wrong with Tom Waits?"

"You don't listen to Tom Waits on your summer vacation. That's something you do when you are hungover on a Saturday afternoon." We had started off this way, Marina and I, picking on each other's music taste. We just couldn't help it. Well, there were many things we couldn't help.

"How about this?" I turned to the next song.

"Is it John Frusciante?"

"Yes, baby."

"I like him, but you know his solo stuff depresses me."

"Now?"

"Seriously? Dinosaur Jr.?"

"Look, I downloaded a few tracks by Paco de Lucía for the occasion."

"Praise the lord," she sighed. We drove all the way down Costa del Sol. It was a three-hour-something ride according to Google Maps. We took a quick break at a service station halfway, had both a *bocadillo de jamon* and smoked a cigarette.

We arrived at our destination in the early afternoon and the entire place appeared semi-deserted. We walked down a narrow alley that led to the beachfront and found the house number of our lodging. A corpulent woman opened the front door, rubbing her drowsy eyes.

"*Bienvenidos*, come in." She kissed the two of us on both cheeks. "I am Maria, the tenant. *Que gusto* to have you. You must be Tony, right?

Oh look at you," she said to Marina in Spanish. "You got yourself a gorgeous one." She winked at me.

"He isn't too bad either," Marina said; somehow her Spanish sounded more real than mine.

"I will show you the apartment," Maria said.

The front door led to a patio that was shared by other households, each of them with the door wide open and we could glimpse their simple furniture. From one of the small apartments a television echoed throughout the patio. I couldn't make much sense of what that TV program was about, but a low male voice was talking to a female voice about why he had to make such a drastic choice and that he did it only for the kids. "Antonio, *por favor*, stay a little longer," begged the female voice. What a tormented man that Antonio must have been, I thought. As we followed Maria to our apartment, the sound intensified. We couldn't see the television through the open door of that apartment but we could see a corpulent elderly woman with a patch on her left eye quietly enjoying the show from her couch, her face in apprehension to find out what would have been Antonio's next move. She noticed us walking by her door. "*Buenos dias*," I said.

"*Buenos dias*," she replied cheerfully and turned back to her program. No one seemed annoyed by the volume of that television.

It was a simple apartment that presented the essentials for a six-day stay, yet Marina and I felt it was more equipped than our apartment back in Wedding. At least the surrounding was more charming, which doesn't say a lot as we are talking about the Wedding District. The walls were adorned by photos depicting the local fisheries, and others flamenco dancers. On a shelf were several poetry books by Rafael Alberti. There were also other Spanish speaking authors, of which I only recognized García Lorca, and even a copy in Spanish of Hemingway's *The Sun also Rises*.

"If you need anything, feel free to knock next door. Here are your keys." Maria gave a big smile and walked off.

We napped and took a shower.

It was about 7 pm when we left the apartment. The elderly woman who was watching TV when we arrived was now sitting on a chair in the patio next to her door.

"*Buenas tardes*," she cheerfully greeted us again.

"*¡Buenas tardes!*"

"*Chicos*," Maria waved at us from her apartment, "how do you like the apartment?"

"*Nos encanta*," I said. Marina nodded with a smile.

"José," Maria called to an old man emerging from the front door and slowly walking toward us, "these are the new guests."

"*Mucho gusto*," we greeted him.

"*Igualmente*," he replied. He looked like someone who had returned from one or two sips. He had a thick head of silver hair and a white beard that looked even more white on his tanned skin.

Then he mumbled something in a strong Southern Spanish dialect. Among the few words and adverbs I was able to discern, one was *pescaito frito* and the other *manzanilla*, hence I assumed he meant to advise us on some restaurant in the vicinity as his arm was pointing at the left of the front door. Perhaps the same he was returning from.

I nodded enthusiastically to show him that his tips were more than welcome and that I was already getting the hang of the Southern Spanish way of speaking.

José looked at me startled and mumbled something before walking toward Maria's house with his unhurried pace. He must have been a handsome man in his prime as Marina pointed out.

"You know I am all about the Mediterranean type," she teased. "You wouldn't have had a chance were you blond."

"I'll better keep an eye on you," I said.

She had that smile of hers. We kissed.

We walked toward the main Plaza at the Casco Historico. Siesta time was past and a crowd of people flooded the entire place. Kids ran after each other, while their parents sat at the terraces of the several bars and restaurants that encircled the Plaza. We saw a free table and sat at it. A young, thin man with long hair sat on a stool next to the steps of a small church and began tuning his acoustic guitar, while another man and a woman helped another woman with her flamenco dress. The show was about to begin.

A waitress approached our table. "What do I bring you?" she asked in Spanish.

"A glass of white," I said in Spanish.

"The same," Marina said.

"Anything to eat?" asked the waitress with a hoarse voice.

"Do you have a menu?" I asked.

"*Claro*," she handed it to me.

"*Pescado frito*?" I asked Marina who agreed with my pick.

The waitress walked back to the bar.

"You want to know what's funny?" Marina asked me.

"What's funny?" I said while lighting a cigarette.

"You have lived for almost four years in Berlin and all you can say is '*ein Bier und ein Kebab mit scharfe Soße.*' Here you act as if you are determined to obtain honorary citizenship."

"It's all about language affinity. Besides, I spend eight hours a day in an office and the time I have left is dedicated to you."

She gave me that disbelieved look she always gave when I tried to find justifications for the fact that I hadn't yet learnt German.

The flamenco show began.

"Do you see any of your fellow citizens?" I asked Marina.

"I have seen no one dipping shrimps into their cappuccino," she said. "It's all clear from here."

We sat for all the duration of the show. We ordered one more glass of wine each, then agreed on simply ordering the entire bottle. In the process the same waitress with the hoarse voice brought us different types of tapas that included olives, seafood, and cuttlefish *croquetas*. At the other tables close to ours we could only hear people speaking Spanish yet we didn't feel out of place. They ate, smoked, talked to each other and laughed, and yet all the bustle didn't interfere with the flamenco show that was now reaching its climax. It was as if all the people, the entire setting, including the kids that chased each other not too distant from the performers, were part of the show. There was a harmony in all of that that one struggles to find elsewhere.

We paid and tipped the waitress and walked through the narrow alleys with their charmingly decadent houses and restaurants and bars in which people, a tide of people, drank, talked, and enjoyed their time. Every alley, every corner and every plate affixed on those walls recounted the relation of those folks with the sea.

We walked as the sound of the tide embraced us until we reached the seaward-facing walls. There were several cannons facing seaward which gave the idea that they hadn't been placed there for ornamental reasons back in the day. About half of them had been removed and the now empty gunports served as windows to the ocean. We leaned out of one of those gunports for some time. It was past midnight.

"How about we get back to the apartment and get some rest for tomorrow?"

"Sure," I said.

The following morning Marina decided to have a look at the city museum. The entry was free, and we started from the archeology section which included for the most parts coins forged by the first settlers and also objects of daily routine including combs, hammers, bracelets, hatchets, knives, earrings, yokes, pots and, it goes without saying, a considerable amount of fishing equipment. The art section was perhaps the most interesting, with paintings by Ruben, El Greco, and even a temporary exposition of Goya's *Pinturas negras.* Those goats were quite something.

"I have read somewhere he painted it as a protest against the inquisition…" Marina said.

"No one expects the Spanish inquisition!"

"… and a satire on the credulity of the people in those times."

"The guy wouldn't lack material these days… look at that tiny dog!"

We then moved to the contemporary art section.

"I think I am going to have the runs," I said.

"You shouldn't have had coffee with that lemon muffin for breakfast," Marina said.

"I don't think it's because of that. Besides I have never had a muffin that good in my entire life. You know contemporary art causes me discomfort."

"And you have the runs when you feel discomfort?"

"My body has to expel the discomfort from somewhere."

"It's not all that bad," Marina said.

"Like that guy you took me to see a few months ago. Big deal, he performed a liposuction on a whale and plugged a lightbulb into a lemon. I should have another of those lemon muffins."

"It's not about the piece per se, it's about the idea behind it. Had anyone thought of doing that before him?"

"My friend Arturo from mid school kept sticking a lightbulb into everything he could find: citrus fruits, vegetables, text books, you name it. No one dared to leave their lunchbox unattended."

"What?"

"He had an electric shock when he was a small kid. He couldn't help it."

"What kind of place did you grow up in?"

"Spooky, isn't it?"

There were some pieces that were not bad. One represented a man, who in reality was not a man but a gnashing human head attached to the body of a dog and being tied by the neck to a kennel which, if you took a closer look at it, was actually a television. And the meaning of it was obvious even for me, even though all I kept seeing was the head of that man being replaced by mine and a computer screen showing pictures of bloggers instead of the television. Those bloggers had done bad to me.

We took lunch at the mercado central which had something mystical, or perhaps Marina was right and that lemon muffin had given me food poisoning which was slowly making its way to my nervous system.

Anyhow, as we crossed the Roman gate that served as the main entrance of the market, it was like entering a baroque cathedral, but instead of the sacred relics covering the tables there was an array of dead fishes, sharks with grinding teeth which I imagined only until a few hours earlier had happily roamed the Atlantic Ocean, shellfish and any sort of sea products one can imagine. And instead of the observants were hordes of men and women intent on making a good deal with the vendors to ensure a fresh and savory meal for dinner. The market was the beating heart of the city and also the place where you could get an abundant plate of fresh local delicacies accompanied with a glass of wine for a few euros.

We sat at a small table, savoring the food and the wine, contemplating that place and the people in it. It's all about finding your own place in the world and I wouldn't blame anyone who would choose that particular one. I began picturing myself and Marina waking up in the morning in our little house at the beachfront. No more public transports, winter coats and emails from fashion bloggers. Just me, Marina, and the sound of the waves. Now, that was a picture.

After siesta, we paid a visit to the beach. It was a small beach delimited by two sea fortresses. One on each side.

We took a swim and then lazed on the sand. For being the nearest beach to the city center, as a matter of fact it must have been a hundred meters away from it; it was quiet. People bathed or talked on the shore; others read books or played with their kids. Some of those people were the same I had seen at the Plaza the night before.

"Look, that's the old lady who sat at the table next to ours yesterday."

"That's the pharmacist."

"How do you know?"

"It's the pharmacy at the corner between the square and the street of our apartment. I saw her as we walked past this morning."

"Shall we have a look at the fortress?" Marina suggested.

"That's a long hike up there."

"Your lust for life amazes me. Are you going to spend the next five days sprawled here?"

"You know I'm perfectly capable of it."

"I know you are perfectly capable of it," she aped me. "We are coming back tomorrow."

"All right, let's go," I said.

The fortress stood at the top of a small island connected by a levee. That was quite a hike. At the sides of the levee the fringing reef served as hunting territory for seagulls and other funny looking aquatic birds I had never seen before. As we passed by, a seagull was pecking at a freshly caught fish already partially dismembered. It gave one or two pecks at it as if to make sure the fish was dead, then looked at both sides and pecked again. It went on for some minutes until it must have concluded that the fish was finally dead. Inside the fortress a museum exhibited the works of local young painters, which both Marina and I enjoyed. There was a lighthouse too.

"How about we stay here?" I asked Marina.

"And what are we going to do?"

"We will find something," I said. "You can teach German, Italian or both."

"What are you going to do?"

"I can work freelance. SEO is the real deal nowadays."

"You know I haven't quite got what you do?"

"Neither have I… I could write a book."

"About what?"

"About seagulls hunting techniques in Southern Spain."

"This is a poor area, you said yourself they have a huge unemployment rate."

"Hector told me," I said, "but these folks don't strike me as being poor. They seem rather happy, to be honest. Take that old woman that sits all day watching her *telenovelas*. She may be half blind, have weight issues, but may god strike me down if she is not always in a pleasant mood."

"She is so sweet. *'Buenos dias'*," Marina imitated the voice of the old woman.

"What about José? He looks like a healthy fella for his age. Okay, aside for the booze. But if you ask me, if in forty years I want to be like him or some pale cantankerous old fart roaming Wedding with a stern look, which do you think I would choose? José hands down."

"As far as you know José may be fifty years old."

"Naaa," I said. "People here know how to live. They wake up, spend hours on the beach, eat, sleep, eat again, watch their flamenco, get drunk, make love, and they wouldn't swap their existence with anyone else's."

"Sometimes you act like a cantankerous old fart," Marina said.

"I didn't say I am not. This is why I need to be saved. There might still be hope for me."

"I seriously doubt it," she said, "but perhaps we could give it a try one day."

At least we got to spend the remaining days of vacation as we thought the locals did.

For our last dinner in that place we ordered a quantity of seafood and wine worth a significant chunk of my salary at The Dancing Avocado. But since I was set to become a Dumboo employee, that didn't really matter anymore.

I woke up in the middle of the night and fetched some water in the kitchen. It was unusually hot, and I realized I had sweated copiously. I opened the curtain of the kitchen window to take a look outside. The city had finally gone to sleep. Marina didn't hear me and kept sleeping.

I went out to the patio. Perhaps some marine breeze was all I needed. It was silent and the doors of the other apartments were shut. I opened the front gate and went to the street. Empty. Not a sound. Only the sound of the sea. It was unusually intense. I began walking barefoot in its direction. Passed through the Plaza Central, the cathedral, the mercado central. Not a soul there.

I walked until the seaward walls. The sea was calm now. The sound of the tide breaking at the water's edge could barely be heard and the sea ripples could hardly be seen even under the full moonlight. The ocean was lifeless.

I leaned out of one of the gunports and saw a feeble light on the surface. It was right below a cliff and had pinkish and turquoise shades that dissolved in the sea.

At the edge of the wall I noticed a small door. It was made of iron but the rust and the ocean had corroded it. It squeaked as I opened it. Behind it a narrow rusty staircase led to the underlying waterfront. Once descended, that unusual luminescence became more distinguishable. I went into the water and swam toward the glow. As I got closer, its shape extended and I could see the source of it. A sea cave. The luminescence led me to the mouth of it. I waded into it, not without some effort. The noise of dripping water was all I could hear. I kept wading into that glowing darkness until I came across a set of rocky steps. They were man-made, but the sea had given them a more natural appearance.

I began climbing up those steps and in the process I began hearing another noise that until then I hadn't been able to discern over the sound of dripping water.

As I reached the end of the steps, I entered a narrow passage and that noise became quite distinct. Like a knock which had regular intervals and collided against the hard wet rock. The passage led into the inner part of the sea cave, an extensive subterranean cavern with a circular shape. The beat had become more intense. I was getting closer to the source of it. I crossed the cavern and reached a small gate that led to a smaller section of it.

As I entered, in the distance I saw a figure crouched and swinging an object resembling a rudimentary hammer. The figure was partially brightened by the scant moonlight that made its way through the inside of the cave and stressed its paleness. He was naked except for what remained of a denim overall. His spinal cord bones protruded unnaturally above his ghostly skin, partially covered in slick hair, and his head had a grotesque conical shape. He didn't give any sign of noticing me approaching and kept hammering furiously with one of his elongated arms.

I was only a few meters away when he turned to me and stood on his feet with those long muscular legs. He stood still, looking at me with the hammer in his hand. He was over two meters tall. I was close enough to discern his features. A scarce stack of black hair encircled his conical skull. A formation of tissue mass that must have served as his ears dissolved at the upper part, merging with the nape. He didn't have a nose but another cancerous lump of skin which presented two tiny holes. His staring eyes, inhumanly bulging, seemed to lack pupils.

I stopped walking. We kept looking at each other for an indefinite time.

He then turned his back on me and walked toward a small moldy stool, sat on it, and began rummaging through a rattling box of metal objects. He then extracted from that pile of scrap metal what looked like a shiny iPad. I got closer behind him as he began typing something on it.

He first checked his inbox. There were mostly promotional emails – the Amazon newsletter suggested some flashy pair of Nike running shoes, while Booking.com recommended a romantic escape to Paris. He then had a look at his Facebook feed which showed a video of a dog saying I love you to his owner and another showing the execution of an ISIS prisoner with a butcher knife. We watched it until one of the executioners held the severed head of the prisoner by the hair while the other recited a prayer from the Koran in front of the camera. He then switched to Instagram on which he began swiping through images of good-looking women in bikinis drinking cocktails in different lavish contexts. After that he went to Pornhub. He was into the lesbian genre. After a few videos, he picked a cooking show with Gordon Ramsay on Netflix and began watching it.

We were in the middle of the episode, Gordon Ramsay was screaming at someone, when that creature turned to me. He looked at me in silence with his staring eyes while Gordon Ramsay kept screaming. His unnaturally wide mouth opened, showing a row of tiny, pointed teeth.

"You should go back now," he whispered at last.

"Where?"

The next morning Marina and I finished packing our things and went to say goodbye to Maria.

"We are waiting for you to come back soon." She hugged the two of us warmly. She seemed sad to see us go. The old woman with the patched eye was there too. "Come back for *La Semana Santa*," she said with her usual cheerful voice.

We had breakfast at a bar in the Plaza Central. I ordered espresso and one of those lemon muffins I knew I would miss dearly.

And off we went to Berlin again.

*

"My name is Leonard and my hobby is making money," the bald man introduced himself while we sat across from him at the table.

Next to him sat this squared guy. His head was squared and had this military haircut and wore very small glasses. His torso was squared too, or perhaps rectangular.

Next to me were four or five newbies who had been invited to attend the first part of the onboarding, called the CEOs' Breakfast. An opportunity for us to get to know the founders of the company, ask questions, and discuss the future of the travel industry. Orange juice, fruit, and croissants on the company.

"How did you come up with the idea of founding Dumboo?" asked one of the newbies.

"We wanted to offer an unique approach to traveling, give the possibility to get to know the places you visit through the eyes of a local."

"Aren't you concerned about the launch of similar platforms?" asked another. "Only in Berlin two were launched this year. How are we going to cope with them?"

"To be honest, I am not concerned about them," Leonard said. "Take 8lodge, for instance, they are about as old as we are but haven't gained any market share in the last two years. In fact, they might shut business any moment."

"What about Buzzstay?" Buzzstay was their biggest competitor, aside from being the first to come up with this lodging thing. I had read of people saying that Dumboo was nothing more than a copycat of them.

"We will get there eventually," replied Leonard, "and it might happen sooner than we think, at least in Europe. In Germany, Austria, and Switzerland we are already outselling them. It is only a matter of time before people, even in America, realize that we are the ones that will take the market to the next level."

"What is it exactly that differentiates Dumboo from our American competitor Buzzstay?" I asked.

Leonard looked at me, then turned to the squared man next to him. "You want to answer this?"

"Isn't that obvious? We are cheaper and offer a better user experience," the squared man said.

I nodded.

"It's about execution," the squared man added. "We believe this is our biggest advantage over them. We are backed by Platypusnetic, which provides an extremely valuable network of experienced professionals in fields such as marketing and IT."

"Any more questions?" Leonard asked.

There was silence.

When does a startup cease to be a startup and becomes an established company? It seemed that Dumboo was in a grey zone.

The folks working in that company gave me blurry or even discordant answers. For some, it had to be considered as an established company, since it had been around for five years and employed over one hundred people, while others still saw it as a startup.

Startup or not, Dumboo had money. Money that came from Platypusnetic and other big investors, and the marketing team alone employed over thirty people.

The Italian team was the smallest, counting only me and Alessandra.

"Can you give me the password for the stock photos?" I asked Alessandra one day. It must have been my second week, and I needed those photos for an article I was writing about Lisbon. I had never been to Lisbon.

"I'm busy now. Didn't I give it to you?" she replied. I glimpsed her screen. She was looking at some Instagram page about tattoos.

In two weeks I had got used to her mood swings. They would go by the day. One day I would sit at my desk and say good morning to her and she would give me a grim look as if I had just yelled at her something like "Pantera is overrated and, by the way, you don't fool me behind those layers of makeup, you're just a career oriented, insecure, money and status driven brat," while the following day she would congratulate with me for a pair of sneakers I was wearing. "Nice shoes, where did you get them? I want to buy the same for my boyfriend."

PLEASE, TELL ME MORE ABOUT YOUR BOYFRIEND.

Every time I was forced to speak to her it was like flipping a coin, and I tried to do so only when Santi was not around to help. Anyhow, this was a bad day for her moods.

"Yes, you did. But there are several other programs for which I received a password. This one must have slipped out. Do you mind giving it to me again?"

"There you go." She wrote the password on a Post-it. "By the way, why don't you look it up on the Google spreadsheet where we keep the login info for all our programs?"

"What spreadsheet?" I asked.

"The one I just told you about," she sighed. "I have sent it to you via Skype." She had greenish eye shadow that morning. She would choose the tones based on the clothes she wore on a particular day. She was pale, sickly pale. And she hated me. Her gaze screamed, *I HATE YOU, I HATE YOU, I HATE YOU!*

"Let me check," I said. I read through all the Skype messages and emails she had sent me for the onboarding. No trace of it. "I don't find it anywhere," I said.

"That's impossible," she said and began typing at her computer. In the meantime I had forgotten the whole matter and returned to my task.

"It seems I forgot to send you that particular file," she said after a while. Her tone had softened but her gaze still screamed hatred. "There you go," she said and sent me the file via Skype.

"No worries, thanks for sending it out," I said and stood up to go fetch some water from the cafeteria. I needed to get out of there. A couple of minutes would do. I could try to take a dump after that. Buy some time. That sounded like a good idea. Sitting the entire day next to that woman caused me discomfort. Perhaps *discomfort* is not the right word. It's something deeper, less tangible. How about *Weltschmerz*? That's it, *Weltschmerz is the word.*

"What's up, Pedro?" Karim asked me as I walked by his desk, heading to the cafeteria.

"I'm Tony," I said. "Pedro sits there," I pointed at a guy on the Spanish team. I heard Alessandra burst into a violent, squawky laughter. Even her laughter caused me *Weltschmerz.* Jesus Christ. *Weltschmerz.* What a grand word.

"You white boys look all the same to me," Karim said.

I grinned. Pedro from the Spanish team didn't take it well. He looked at me from behind his screen and rolled his eyes. We didn't look much alike, I thought.

"How is it going?" Karim asked. He always wore that baseball cap, even when he sat at his desk, as a disguise for the galloping hair loss.

"Great, I feel I'm catching up quickly," I said.

Karim was our CMO, which means that Santi and the other team leaders of the marketing department had to report to him. He used to be the Head of SEO, and after his promotion, he hired Santi to take his place. It was rumored that the previous CMO had got a job at a well-known e-commerce company but Leonard and the squared man wouldn't let him go before finding a fitting replacement. In order to be released from his contract, he recommended that Karim would take his place despite the fact that Karim was known in the company for his incompetence and dubious work ethic. As a result Karim found himself managing a team of over thirty people and with a six-digit yearly salary fattening his bank account.

Karim had a thing for expensive watches and every time he purchased one he would come to one of us and say something like, "Dude, check this, guess how much?"

"Don't know, 300 hundred?" I guessed one day as he asked me.

He looked at me with disbelief. "Seven grand," Karim said proudly, adjusting the thing on his wrist. "I bet I am the only here who can afford it."

I heard someone in the room muttering outraged, "WHAT?" "Bloody fuckwit," exclaimed someone with a British accent. Another stood up noisily and walked out of the room.

*

It was the squared man's birthday. He himself brought a cake to the office that morning. A huge cake and with it came what looked like a miniaturized soothing waterfall. Not sure what the waterfall stood for. He dragged two desks to the center of the room and placed them next to each other, and on top of them he placed the cake and, next to the cake, the waterfall which had real flowing water and tiny trees. Then he began to inflate balloons and gave two interns the order to help him with that. Without saying a word, they both stood up and began inflating those balloons. Our colleague, Mathilde, helped him with the glasses, plates and cutlery, making sure everything was in the right place. Mathilde dressed differently than the other women in the marketing team. She had a thing for high heels and business suits.

Then the squared man began passing by the desks and asked people to join his celebration. For some reason, he only asked the women and the department heads like Karim; Santi was ignored, like the rest of us.

A bottle popped and they began singing the happy birthday song.

"Why didn't we get invited?" whispered someone from the French team.

"Because we don't have boobs," said Pedro from the Spanish team.

"I do have boobs," whispered Michelle from the British team.

"Yes, but you're a lesbian," said Liam who worked in the same team.

"What's the cake like? What's the cake like?" asked the same guy from the French team.

"Why don't you go check?" Pedro suggested.

"Assuming that lesbians are unwelcome, if he sees a gay man

getting too close to his cake, he will at least beat him with a stick," the French guy said.

"I will go," said Pedro. "I will pretend to go talk to Beatriz at the far end of the room." Beatriz was our graphic designer.

Pedro walked by the gathering and peeked at the cake. Then he reached Beatriz's desk and I saw them laughing and looking at the gathering of people, then he returned to his desk with the same furtive pace.

"Well?" Liam asked.

"It's him," Pedro said.

"What do you mean *him*?"

"It's him on the cake," Pedro said. "He had the pastry shop print a photo of himself on the cake."

"Jesus," Michelle exclaimed. "By the way, Tony, well done with Gollum the other day." Gollum was the nickname they had given to Karim, it had something to do with his bulging eyes and bald head.

"What did I do?"

"Did that look like a 300-quid watch to you?"

"Maybe," I said. "I don't know much about watches."

"I can see that," she giggled, pointing at the torn canvas bracelet on my wrist. "Well, the face he made when you said 300 was priceless." She turned to Pedro. "What is Alexander turning?" Alexander was the squared man's name.

"Thirty-one," said Pedro.

"WHAT?" Santi shouted. Being our team leader he tried not to be involved in those chit-chats, although it usually didn't take long before we managed to drag him in.

"Bullshit," Liam said. "He can't be younger than me."

"How old are you Liam?" Michelle asked.

"Thirty-two. I have a four-year-old daughter and, despite that, I have a fresher look than this guy."

"You would have an even fresher look if you would quit smoking." Michelle giggled. "Do you believe having a child is harder work than running a company?"

"Hands down," Liam said.

"How old are you Santi?" Michelle asked.

"30," said Santi.

"Fuck," cried Liam. "Am I the oldest in this place?"

Mathilde walked back to her desk. The birthday party was over. She had made a flower crown the day before and placed it on top of the squared man's squared head, "What were you talking about?" she asked us.

"Liam thinks he is the oldest in the company."

"How old are you, Liam?" Mathilde asked.

"Thirty-two," he said looking at his screen.

"Leonard is thirty-four," Mathilde said. "Also Jannik from Data and Erik from Customer Support are past thirty-five. Karim is thirty-six."

"How come you know all their birthdays?" Michelle asked her, not without a hint of malice.

Mathilde didn't reply and sat on her desk. We all got back to our duties.

When I returned home I told Marina about the squared man, the cake, and the waterfall with the tiny trees.

She was having a hard time making sense of what I was telling her. At first she thought I referred to this guy simply being really German.

"I'm telling you," I insisted, "this guy is really squared."

"But he must at least have some human features. There are no such things as squared people," she said as if she couldn't believe she was actually having this conversation. She too had to endure her fair share of oddities at work. A visitor to the museum that day had taken a dump into a urinal. They had to print a guide in English and a bunch of other languages on how to properly use a urinal. Then they hung it at the entrance of the men's room.

"He is like a bunch of wooden blocks stacked on top of each other," I said. "You know, those they give toddlers to play with?"

"Have you smoked or something?" she asked me.

"I haven't," I said while opening the laptop and googling the squared man's name. "Do we still have some?" I asked her.

"I thought you wanted to go straight with the new job," Marina said.

"How about we finish the one we have, then we take a break?" I proposed.

"Sounds about right to me," she said and went to fetch a small plastic bag inside a beauty box. She began undoing a cigarette and mixed the tobacco with the weed.

"There you go," I said, and showed her a picture of the squared man I had found on LinkedIn

"Fuck," she couldn't believe what she was seeing. "He is really squared."

*

Almost a year had gone by and I was still at Dumboo. The job was easy, not too different from what I did at The Dancing Avocado. There was the link-building but instead of the fashion bloggers, I had to annoy the travel counterparts which turned out to be even more cocky. Still, I found less discomfort looking at their smiley images taken in different corners of the world. I also got to write about places.

"Tony, my man, do you have a ciggy for me?" Liam asked one day as I was about to finish an article about the Cyclades. I had never been to the Cyclades either.

"There you go," I handed him my pack.

"Sick. Want to smoke with me?"

"Sure," I followed him.

He walked past the front door, "I thought you wanted to go downstairs," I said.

"I know a better place."

We walked to the men's room. He opened the stall at the far end of the row, stepped on top of the toilet, opened a small window that looked on the backyard, and disappeared through it. Liam was a skinny fella but a lot taller than me. Our office was on the seventh floor. The seventh floor, for Christ's sake, and I thought that was a lousy way to go. I could picture the headlines in the next day's newspapers.

UNDERPAID ITALIAN MARKETER OF A NOTORIOUS BUSINESS CLONE JUMPS OUT OF THE BATHROOM WINDOW ON THE SEVENTH FLOOR. ANGELA MERKEL CALLS FOR REGULARIZATIONS OF SMOKING AREAS IN WORKPLACES.

"Come on out," Liam said sticking his head in.

I stepped on the toilet and had a look out of the small window. All I saw was the nothingness. *The fuck I am coming out*, I said to myself.

"Don't chicken out on me, Tony," Liam said, laughing.

I stood on my tiptoe and took a better look. There was an eave right below the window. It must have been two meters wide. Liam sat cozily on it, building a joint using the cigarette I gave him. I climbed out the window and sat next to him. I didn't dare to look at what lay beyond the edge of the eave. "Do you come here often?" I asked him.

"Sick, isn't it?" He took two hits and handed me the joint. "Say, Tony, you think Leicester is going to make it?"

"How many games are left?"

"Seven… I think."

"City is out of the game. And Tottenham is not going to win anytime soon. I'm not even considering the Gunners."

"I will tattoo Ranieri's name next to my daughter's."

"How old is she?"

"Almost five. It's a good age," he said before taking out his phone and showed me a video of his daughter dancing to a song by The Jam in their living room.

"She is already into the good music," I said.

"Yeah, we better educate them from the start. Next thing you know they hang up a bloody Maroon 5 poster in their room."

"God forbid," I said while inhaling the smoke.

"What about you?"

I gave a dry laugh and coughed. "Hell no, it's not a good time."

"It's never a good time."

"Were you already working here when you had her?" I asked him.

"No, we had just moved to Berlin. I was freelancing for some newspapers and music magazines back in the UK. My wife had found a job here, she is in fashion, and I followed her. When we got the news, I figured I needed something more stable. And look where I am now." He laughed bitterly.

We finished the joint and returned to our desks. I never returned there to smoke, unlike Liam.

Some time later, Santi told me that one day Stefan, the Head of Finance, was quietly sitting on the toilet doing his business, when suddenly he saw Liam's face appearing from the window. Stefan must haven't been aware of the eave on which Liam used to spend his cigarette breaks and, in shock and without wiping his ass, he pulled up his trousers and ran away. That same day Liam approached him, threatening him to not tell anyone. Of course, Stefan never spoke about the incident to anyone.

Anyway, that joint I had just had with Liam quickly got to my head. It was 5 pm and I thought that, if I were lucky, no one would talk to me in the remaining hour.

That is exactly what happened a few minutes after I returned to my seat.

"Hey Tony, check this out." Santi asked me to take a look at his computer. It showed a line graph.

"What's this?" I asked, trying to sound as restrained as I could.

"This is Buzzstay…" he pointed at a line, "and this is us," he said, pointing at another line that pulled ahead. "In the last year we have killed them," he said with that big excited smile of his. "Tony, are you ok?" He gave me an amused look. He was a clever guy.

"I am fine, why?" I then tried to get back to the subject. "But they are still ahead in overall visibility."

"Sure, they are the big brand. But if people google something like lodging in Paris, Rome, London, or whatever, in most cases they see us first. In the SEO game we are doing a better job than them."

"Does it mean we all get a raise?"

He chuckled. "I don't think so," he said, "not for now at least. But this proves that we are doing a great job. Let's keep it up."

"Yessir!"

"I have something for you," he said.

"You bought me a present?"

"Yeah, more weed," he chuckled again. "Would you like to be in charge of our next campaign? The new season of *Dragon Lore* is coming out. I think we should come up with something big. You know, to take advantage of the media coverage it is going to unleash."

"I agree, all kinds of media are going to talk about it."

"So, do you want to take care of it?" Santi asked.

"Sure, why not?" I replied. "*Gracias* Santi."

"I know you will do a good job. One thing though. If I were you I would start working on a draft *asap,* but I wouldn't spread the news with the others."

"May I ask why?"

"If Mathilde finds out I gave it to you she will go to Alexander and complain. And I don't want Alexander on my balls again, after the fiasco of the last campaign."

"Understood, thanks for the heads up."

I didn't share Santi's enthusiasm for digital marketing, not even close, and more than once I suspected that this guy must have suffered from some nasty mental condition to show such dedication for these people, despite all the shit they made him endure. Yet, for some obscure reason, I knew that I couldn't have possibly forgiven myself had I ever, even involuntarily, disappointed this man. I did my best to prevent that from happening.

Some might have even said I had become some sort of an overachiever. Who would have thought?

*

I began working on the campaign. Marina helped me with it. We used to watch *Dragon Lore* together and I thought she could have made a better marketer than I.

Each scene of the show was shot in some alluring amphitheater, medieval castle, or volcanic scenery around Europe and the show was known for dragging masses of travelers, Instagramers, and selfie sticks from all over the globe to inundate those places.

In each of those places we had listings and what better way to live your favorite show than staying in one of Dumboo's unrivaled lodgings? The approach was solid but that had already been done by our competitors. I needed something more.

Santi advised me to go talk to this Italian guy from the Data team. He was the work-hard-play-hard type, top-tier private university in Milan, who would show up at work with Google Glasses and a white shirt and end the day doing cocaine in some high-class strip club. Those times we would bump into each other in the office he would say something like, "What's up, Tony? Let's talk about bitcoins."

"Why?" would be my usual answer.

So I went to this guy, "Hey, Marco. What's up buddy? Would you mind giving me some numbers concerning the bookings we received in the destinations I have on this list?" I handed him the printed list. "2015 versus 2016 if possible. This way I can calculate the difference."

"Sure," he said. "I can give them to you next Wednesday."

"It's rather urgent," I said, "and Santi mentioned it should take no more than five minutes."

"All right then," he opened his data software, "is this what you're looking for?"

"Exactly what I am looking for, thanks buddy," I said. "Wait, I don't see any data concerning Norway in 2015."

"That is because we didn't have a sufficient volume of bookings that year to be computed by the software."

"That's a bummer," I said. "I am working on something big, and I am making a year-to-year comparison of our bookings. Journalists love this stuff and would give us lots of visibility in exchange for using it," I said.

"Why don't you make up those numbers?" he suggested.

"Can I?"

"Sure, as long as it looks realistic."

"Wouldn't it cause us trouble?"

"It's our internal data. Only we have access to it."

"Solid, thanks again," I said. "Let me know whenever you're up for that chat about bitcoins. I think I might have a knack for it."

He grumbled and returned to his business.

It took over one week of writing and data elaboration. Beatriz, our Spanish designer, created a nice stylized map and data charts that invoked the look of the tv show. It took another day for the translators to translate it for all our markets. I had almost the entire marketing team working on that project, and I have to admit, it felt good to have all those people following my directives. I even thought I was good at it. Perhaps I was destined to become a great team leader one day who, in turn, would inspire the leaders of the future.

The campaign worked like a charm. LinkedIn turned out to be the perfect honeypot for journalists in search of a good story to sell to their editors. And we went for the biggest publications in Italy, Germany, France, UK, Spain and so on. Within two days, the Dumboo brand appeared on half of the major digital publications in Europe. The piece had gone viral. Little did they know that the numbers about Norway were fabricated and that we had even inflated some of the 2016 numbers to show the increase in bookings.

Karim approached Santi and tossed three tickets on his desk.

"What's that?" Santi asked him.

"We have received three passes to attend the Magical Mystery Search Engine Fest this Thursday evening."

"Cool," Santi said. "This year it is going to be held in Berlin."

"You're expected to go," Karim said, "and choose two others from the team to go with you. Oh, wait a minute," he said before grabbing one of the tickets and placing it on Mathilde's desk. "Mathilde is going with you. You can choose another from your team."

"Aren't you going?" Santi asked Karim.

"No," Karim hesitated. "I have things to do that day." He then walked off.

After a while Santi called over to me, "Tony, could you please come over?"

I walked to his desk.

"Dude, I need to pick someone from the team to go to the Magical Mystery Search Engine Fest."

"What is it?" I asked.

"Man, it's the biggest digital marketing conference in Europe. All the big industry names are going to be there. They all give speeches and share some of their magic. Wanna come with me?"

"Thanks buddy," I said. "Isn't there anyone else who would like to go?"

"I wanted to check with you first. It'll be cool. They have free beer," he said all excited as if we were going to Burning Man instead.

"Alright," I said.

"By the way, Mathilde is coming too."

So we went that Thursday afternoon. Santi, Mathilde, and I.

"I am so excited," Mathilde began quivering as we waited in line to enter the exhibition ground. "I so wanna meet Rory Fisherman. He is such an inspiration," she cried and gripped my forearm. She was one of those people who always need to get hold of some body parts when they talk to you.

Santi gave Mathilde and me our badges to wear during the conference. I looked at mine. Karim had sent the wrong information to the organizers and so, for that day, I was Pedro La Matina, born somewhere between the Strait of Gibraltar and the Cyclades.

We got in and the first thing I saw was this stand where they sold the conference's merchandise. T-shirts and mugs for the most part. The t-shirts' printings read things like, *100% Organic; Keep Calm and SEO; Born to be a Marketer; Sex, Drugs and SEO; SEO is not Dead; Eat, Sleep, SEO, Repeat; Gotta Link?; Baby Got Links; I'd Rather be on TOP; A SEO guy died while crossing a road, why? Too much traffic.*

Something felt terribly wrong at that moment. It really did.

We entered the main conference hall and took our seats. A hostess walked by the attendees and handed each of us a pair of 3D glasses. Not like those they give you at the theater when you are watching some Christopher Nolan movie. Those were thicker, heavy plastic. I shook mine and heard cables and circuits rattling inside it. Then the presenter came on stage and told us to download the conference app. This way we would be able to ask real time questions to the speaker by simply using our phones.

"What do we need these for?" I asked Santi.

"I think we will be able to see the questions people write to them while they speak, like in a chat room."

Mathilde and Santi put them on. I decided against it for the beginning of the conference.

The first speaker got on stage. A woman. She had founded a company in New York City, something to do with interior design. She began talking about lead generation. Gain the trust of your customers, educate them, create a funnel bla-bla-bla. Then she talked about her company's success story for the rest of the time, before concluding with a praise for SEOKing, a well-known marketing analytics software which was the main sponsor of the event.

"It's by far the best and most all-round marketing software out there," she insisted.

The previous year, the conference's main sponsor was OzSEO, SEOKing's main competitor. The same speaker was there too and I wondered if she said that OzSEO was the best and most all-round marketing software out there too.

She then introduced the next speaker, "A brilliant mind and a great friend of mine," before leaving the stage.

It was a hipster-type from Germany who founded something about bike sharing. Same story. He talked about leveraging your team, influencing your audience, then there was a fifteen minutes promo of his company – "SEOKing is the best tool out there" – and at last he introduced the next speaker, "outstanding guy, a real inspiration."

The same pantomime went on with the following speakers. It then occurred to me these people had it all figured out. They were all part of a big apparatus in which they needed each other to be legitimized. A perfect engine which aliments itself. *You advertise me and I will be glad to advertise you in turn*. But they needed us, the audience. They needed us to buy their products, put a 'Like' on their Facebook page, become subscribers of their newsletter, buy their books about marketing strategies, use their fucking marketing software. But most of all, they needed us to aliment their egos. Make them feel like the real rockstars of the twenty-first century. They already had a taste of it so they needed more. They knew that without the perfect engine of which they were a part, they would spend their meaningless lives playing shooter games, eating tortilla chips, and making cyber-love to each other.

After about seven hours of this, interrupted by an hour and a half lunch break, it was time for the highlight of the conference. The headliner, the real rockstar, the symbol of the whole movement.

Rory Fisherman came on stage with his arms raised toward the audience. He wore a black leather jacket and sported a Dali-like mustache. The entire hall burst into a standing ovation before he could even say anything.

He began his speech and I decided to give the 3D glasses a try. I put them on and began listening to this guy. He talked about his company, shared some of his strategies with the audience. The whole pantomime.

I began to feel dizzy. My head began spinning and I felt numbness in my limbs. I felt like shivering.

The 3D glasses highlighted Rory's facial features. Right next to his face were the questions the audience kept sending. I kept looking at him behind those glasses and realized something was not right. Rory looked sick, extremely sick. He had purplish circles under his eyes and his cheeks were covered with purulent nodes, spurting some greenish liquid. Something creeped under his skin, trying to break out. There was something wrong about his body too. His arms began to swell beneath his leather jacket and something was coming out the bottom of his skinny jeans, slithering appendages that began to spread around the stage, reaching for the audience.

The audience was changing too. Slowly. I turned to my left and saw Santi and Mathilde sitting next to me; they looked like awakened corpses wearing 3D glasses. I raised my hands. I looked at them. I had grey hands with purple, bulging veins.

I took off the glasses. Rory was done. The room burst into another standing ovation. They all looked normal again. So did my hands.

I went out of the room and walked to the refreshment area, drank some water, then cracked a beer open.

Rory Fisherman came out, surrounded by a tide of people, Mathilde was among them. She managed to get close to him and get his attention, then began talking to him and touching his forearm.

I couldn't see Santi. He had disappeared.

I sipped my beer and saw this fat guy approaching me. A tall, chubby guy with no signs of beard growth. He looked like a giant kid. He tried to pull a cool attitude, some James-Bond-kind of cool, finding himself in his natural element.

He placed his flaccid sausage fingers on my shoulder. "What's the best place to hide a dead body?" he asked me.

"WHAT?"

"The second page of Google," he smirked.

I pushed his sausage fingers away. I couldn't tell why, but I felt an irresistible urge to bash that beardless smirky face against the table with the beverages.

I didn't. I just walked out of that place with the beer in my hand.

The day after I called in sick. Marina and I stayed in bed until noon, then had brunch at a café in Prenzlauer Berg. Scrambled eggs and salmon. Took a stroll at a park before returning home. Saturday and Sunday were pretty much the same.

Those were the days when even Berlin looked beautiful.

*

Some days later I walked to my desk and Alessandra was painting her toenails. She was painting them in blue. It was not the first time she had done that right next to me. She was wearing blue eye shadow that day.

I greeted her.

"Hi," she replied without looking in my direction.

I sat down.

"I have something to tell you," she said after a while, still bent at her toenails.

"What's up?"

"I am leaving," she said.

"Uh."

"I talked yesterday with Karim and Santi. I will keep working here for the next two weeks."

"Sorry to hear that," I said.

"Naa, that's fine. It was my decision, anyway."

Do you want to know what's one of the hardest things to do when you work in an office? Finding the right words to say when a person you have always found obnoxious comes to you and says they are leaving. You begin hearing joyful music inside your head and get that foolish feeling that nothing bad can ever happen to you and your career. You're destined for your well-deserved happiness after what you had to endure. All the while that person pronounces those prophetic words, "I AM THE FUCK OUTTA HERE." But of course you can't appear happy about the news, nor even indifferent for that matter. And despite the role playing game you're in, you can't make a scene, pretending you're crushed by that news and hug that person. Which is what most people do, anyway.

Therefore my reaction came across as indifferent simply because I didn't have a clue of what to say or do. I was surprised, that's all.

"There is something else you should know," she said.

"What's that?"

"They won't hire anyone to replace me, since they think you can handle the Italian market on your own… Obviously!"

Now, I was not sure how to interpret that last *obviously*, pronounced with such emphasis. Either as mockery, implying that I had been left alone to deal with that hot potato and it was now a matter of time before things will begin falling apart around me, or it was her way to admit that, after all, I was good at my job, perhaps even better than her, and another rooster in the hen house would have just worked against the interests of the Italian market.

Of course, the simplest explanation had to do with money, as one salary on the payroll is more welcome than two. So let's get rid of the moody satanist and exploit this clueless idiot until he burns out!

What a win-win situation Karim must have smelled there.

Not everyone was happy about the *Dragon Lore* project. Mathilde didn't lose time to show her frustration for not having been assigned that project. She went bitching to the squared man about Santi, and the squared man, in turn, demanded Karim take some measure.

Some days after the launch of the campaign, Karim called for Santi.

"I am not happy about how you dealt with the last campaign," Karim told Santi, not minding the fact everyone in the room could hear. Or perhaps he wanted everyone to hear.

"Could you be more specific?" Santi replied.

"First of all, why wasn't I informed about this project?

"I am responsible for the main content projects," Santi said.

"Yes, but I would have preferred you telling me about it beforehand," Karim began yelling.

"I don't understand what's wrong with it. It's the best piece of content marketing we have ever created in this company and it's giving us lots of visibility for free."

That was the first time I saw Santi getting upset. His head turned flaming red, which contrasted with the grey of his beard and hair. But hey, you should have seen how he stood his ground. He walked back to his desk and grabbed his laptop before returning to Karim. "Look, the biggest newspapers, respectively in Italy and Spain. Look at these two in France and UK." His vehemence made him almost slam the computer against Karim's face. "Even *Vanity Bazaar*! Dude we are talking about the best publications out there."

Karim didn't rebut; he looked startled at Santi's computer.

"And you know how much budget we used?" cried Santi who had now reached the climax of his outburst which, it occurred to me, had not been triggered by Karim's scolding him in this particular moment. That was only the last straw. After months of overtime, reports demanded at the last minute by the CEOs which should have been compiled by Karim who, in turn, dumped them on Santi, and other forms of abuses, that was it. He couldn't accept anyone, not even his boss, disparaging what he considered one of his best achievements as a manager. "Not a cent!" Santi yelled at last.

Karim looked at him, speechless, didn't see what had just hit him. Only after what felt like an eternity did he find the lucidity to mutter, "next time, please, let me know in advance."

                                    *

We kept receiving coverage from the press. Some weeks later, a French TV program aired interviews of angry lodging owners complaining about the indolence of the company toward the frequent cases of vandalism in their properties. During prime time, a woman with her husband displayed the condition of her apartment after a guest decided to throw a party in it. Empty bottles on the floor, cigarette marks on the couch, used condoms on the bathroom floor and a shattered chandelier. At last the camera zoomed in on the rug in the living room which had been set on fire. The guest had disappeared, and they had tried in vain to reach him via telephone or emails.

"And what did Dumboo do?" the reporter asked the woman.

The cameraman zoomed in on the lady's face. "They said their insurance covers only part of the damage and for the rest they can't do anything," she told the camera before showing a copy of the contract to the reporter.

"Do you mind if I make a copy of it?" the reporter asked.

"Go ahead. Whatever it takes to have some justice," the woman said.

A few days later, that same reporter rang our doorbell. "I would like to talk with the CEOs," he said to our office manager with a pronounced French accent. The cameraman behind him had already started recording.

"Please wait here," the office manager walked to the CEOs' office, visibly distressed by the unannounced visit of the French TV crew. As my desk faced the front door, I could hear and see most of what was going on.

While waiting, the reporter began asking questions to everyone who, for any reason, walked by.

"Are you aware of the way your company treats your hosts?" he asked an intern. She was walking to the restroom with her head down and flinched on seeing the microphone raised at her face. "I'm sorry, I'm just an intern," she said.

"In what department do you work?" the reporter insisted. "Do you know anyone I can talk to?"

"Sorry…" she mumbled and walked away.

He then began asking questions to the people sitting at their desks near the entrance. Luckily, I was spared. When the office manager returned, a crowd of people had formed around the reporter. "The CEOs are currently busy," she said, "but they will be happy to arrange another interview under appointment. Now please let us get back to work."

"I only need to ask them a few questions," the reporter said. "It won't take longer than ten minutes."

"I am sorry," the office manager replied and gestured for them to walk out.

"Is there anyone else we can talk to? Anyone from customer service? Operations?"

"No. Now if you please, we have work to do."

"We will wait then."

"You can't wait inside."

"Is this company always so rude with people who demand answers?" the reporter shouted in his French accent, before walking out the door with the cameraman.

No signs from Leonard nor the squared man. As I walked by the entrance, heading to the restroom, I saw the reporter crouched while the cameraman had dropped his camera and was looking at his phone. The reporter waved at me with a cheeky smile. They waited behind the glass door for over an hour.

Then the office manager picked up a call and rushed to the CEOs' office. She returned after a while with the squared man who went straight to the reporter and the cameraman outside. I saw the reporter gesturing at the cameraman to stand up and pick up the camera, then the squared man said something to them, I figured it must have not been a compliment, and walked back inside.

They left soon after and within a few days that report had been seen by millions of people on TV and YouTube.

*

A few months later Santi approached me. "I need to show you something," he said. He had a gloomy look on his face.

He showed me an article recently published in a magazine about digital marketing. It was titled "Amazing Examples of In-House Content Marketing".

"They are talking about the *Dragon Lore* project. This is sick!" I said, I had taken up *sick* from Liam.

"Keep reading," he said.

I read it:

We reached out to Karim Meghni (CMO at Dumboo) to find out more about this great piece of content.

- Interviewer: How did you come up with the idea?

- Karim: We wanted to take advantage of the huge interest in Dragon Lore. We knew that its fan base is big, so we had an audience to reach out to. The season was about to start so we also knew that it would be a hot topic and the publishers could potentially pick up on it. We have additionally created images with facts and statistics with the aim to show how filming Dragon Lore in those destinations has impacted the local tourism. This sort of information is always attractive to journalists.

- Interviewer: What challenges did you face during the production of this campaign?

- Karim: It was very time-consuming to research for the project and to collect all data, stats, information that we needed, however we decided to use the content for different markets. And it was a great success!

Santi and I looked at each other. Not a word. I returned to my seat and got back to my tasks.

Some days later, Santi had regained his usual spirits. "I've got great news."

"What's up?" I asked him.

"Michelle is leaving the company," he said as if Michelle leaving us was the best thing that had happened to him in months.

"I thought you liked Michelle," I said.

"Of course I do, she is great. But you know what it means?"

"Finally someone is showing some self-respect?"

"Perhaps, and that her position is now vacant. And we are now searching for a new Head of Content, and the great news is that for now we will only consider internal applications. Tony, you move your lazy ass and apply. NOW!"

"I am not sure. Karim will take a final decision on that, right?"

"Yes, but I will review the applications too. I will talk to him, that's the least he can do after taking credit for your work."

"I will give it a try," I said more to please him than with the conviction that anything good could come from this.

That night I received a message on Facebook from Anna. I hadn't heard from her since they shut Re-Juvinator.

Hey Tony, how are you? I recently started working with a fitness and health company in Miami that has made two billion dollars in the last three years and they will soon launch in Italy. We are looking for influencers there. We have webinars twice a week that explain the strategy and how they will kick start the Italian market. If you are

I clicked on the link and this guy named Brian appeared on my
screen. Brian was a white male from the US, about forty years old, who
claimed he had lost 60 lbs. thanks to a miraculous body loss program that
involved nutritional products and energy drinks produced by a company
that went by the name of Proteinbozia. Before-and-after photos showed
his body transformation from a curved and afflicted saggy man to a
muscular self-reliant advocate of the American dream. In the video Brian
explained how, after his transformation, he undertook a quest to inspire
other fellow Americans to follow in his footsteps. "Start our sixty day
challenge," he said pointing his finger at the camera, "and not only will
you be finally able to unleash your full potential, but you will impact the
lives of millions around the world. YOUR STORY CAN CHANGE THE
WORLD!"

I left Brian and his self-assurance to find more information about
this sixty day challenge.

If you wanted to stop being a loser and become an inspiration for
millions of other outcasts like you, all you had to do was to answer a
questionnaire, filling in your personal information and the name of the
promoter who referred you. After that Proteinbozia would deliver its
milkshakes to your home and, once you were ready to become the next
Sylvester Stallone, you had to record a video of yourself and blabber
something like, "Challenge accepted! My pal Tucker challenged me to
lose whatever amount of pounds in the next sixty days. Now I challenge
you to do the same." And since Tucker has been such a considerate

friend to you, you were asked to mention his name in the video, so he would get a commission for luring you into this thing. And this luring thing went on and on; the more people you pulled in the more money you made.

I replied to Anna:

Hey Anna, good to hear from you. I hope Florida is treating you well. About the influencer job, I don't think I am the right person for it. I have a hard time influencing my own course of life and I doubt I would be able to influence others to take any reasonable action for themselves. But if I ever change my mind, I will let you know.

Many thanks for the offer, though.

Tony.

She wrote me back the next day

Hi Tony, please find the details for the webinar tonight. It explains the strategy and how the company will open the Italian market below.

Sure, thanks Anna, I replied.

*

Mathilde got the Head of Content job. Too bad for her. Rumors had begun spreading about the company's finances drifting into troubled waters. It started with the video of the French reporter being kicked out of our office going viral on the Internet. Thousands of hosts began removing their properties from our listings.

Everyone knew the shit had hit the fan when Leonard and the squared man laid off the entire French, Dutch, and British teams.

I was smoking in the backyard when Pedro came running. "Karim wants to talk to you," he said.

There I go, I thought. I gave Pedro my unfinished cigarette and he took it gladly, despite not being a smoker. God knew how much he needed it.

I entered a small meeting room. Karim sat there. "Take a seat, Antonio." In one year and a half the son of a bitch had never realized I loathed being called Antonio.

"I want you to know that your position is not at risk and that the company is in good health. What's happening now comes from our decision to shift our resources to the more rewarding markets."

"Is this why you wanted to talk to me?"

"Yes."

"Can I go now?"

"Yes, you can. And Antonio… thanks for your hard work. When the right time comes, I won't forget it."

"Sure, no problem."

I returned downstairs and lit another cigarette. Pedro was still there.

"So?" he asked.

"Please someone explain to me what just happened in there," I said.

"What did he tell you?" Pedro asked.

"He said I have nothing to worry about and that the company is not filing for bankruptcy."

"He said the same to me. They want to keep us quiet."

"Want another cigarette?"

He took it.

We saw a group of people from the French and British teams. They were comforting a girl who was crying. She sobbed, covering her face. "What am I going to do now? Why are they doing this to us?" People from other companies walked by and looked at her startled.

Liam was holding her and his expression said it all. He was a good bass player who had introduced me to the music of Les Claypool. He played in a band. Good shit.

"He should at least have given us some explanations," Liam said to me and Pedro, referring to Karim. "He is so fucking cowardly. I want him to look each of us in the eye and say that we are sacked."

Right at that moment, Karim came out. He had a black hoodie on top of his cap and wore shades. The moment he saw the bunch of us, he hastened his pace. Liam saw him trying to sneak out of the backyard. "Hey Karim, mate, why are you avoiding us? Don't we at least deserve some explanation?" he shouted.

Karim quickly turned around. "Santi has told you everything there is to know," he said and rushed to the exit.

"But I want you to say it to me to my face, or perhaps you don't have the guts. Do you have the guts, Karim?"

Karim kept walking.

"Hey Karim, WAIT A MINUTE, MATE." Liam dashed to him.

Pedro and I looked at each other and went after Liam. I am 1,83 and Pedro was almost as tall, yet Liam outsized us by a head and we barely managed to stop him from bashing Karim's head against one of the parked cars. Karim saw his life flashing before his eyes and ran off. As I gripped Liam's arm, I thought how nice it would have been to lose my grip and let the events take their natural course. I thought Pedro must have felt the same.

Jesus Christ, that Karim could run really fast.

*

Leonard called for a special meeting to reassure everyone about the situation. "The rumors about us facing financial issues are unfounded, nor is it true that Platypusnetic is trying to sell the company, let alone to Buzzstay. The company finances are healthy and Platypusnetic has renewed its commitment to establish this company as the world leader in the lodging industry."

"We are conducting an internal investigation to identify those spreading these false rumors," the squared man took the floor, "these rumors are not only harming me and Leonard as CEOs of this company, they are harming each and every one of you. Therefore we encourage everyone aware of individuals acting against the company's interests, to report directly to me and Leonard."

"How are you, Tony?" Mathilde approached me in the cafeteria after the meeting. "Crazy shit is happening, isn't it?"

"Well, Leonard and the sq…", I paused, "and Alexander said there is nothing we should worry about."

"Do you believe them?" she asked.

"Sure, why not? I just feel sorry for Liam and the others."

"I am sure it was not an easy decision for them to lay off those markets."

I nodded.

"And between us," she lay her hand on my arm, "we both know that in the French and British markets anarchy reigned supreme. They showed up late and left earlier than all of us. Their performance was poor to say the least."

"They will be just fine," I said. Right at that moment Santi walked in and gave me a wary look. He sat at one of the tables.

"See you, Tony," Mathilde walked off.

I walked over to Santi and sat in front of him. "What's up, buddy?"

"Be careful with that one," he said. He gazed dully at his mug. *What have they done to this man?*

"Feel like talking?"

"It was the first time I had to do something like this," he said. "It's not a nice feeling to tell people you consider friends that they are fired."

"They know it was not your decision. You know Liam, next time we go play football I am sure he will join us. He is not the kind of guy who holds grudges. Right now he is likely pitying you for being the poor bastard who had the task to tell them."

That managed to make him smile.

"Let's have a beer after work," I said. "I will ask Liam to join."

"Sounds good."

"I will write to him."

"Tony."

"What?"

"Be careful of what you say to Mathilde."

"What do you mean?"

"In the last week she has been approaching people in the office, me included."

"Did she ask you what you think of this situation?"

"She is asking everyone the same. They are trying to set us up and get rid of as many people as they can. This is only the beginning."

Well, it turned out Santi was right.

One month passed before they began calling us individually for a meeting with the squared man.

They called for Santi and he returned after one hour. "What happened?" I asked him.

"He is asking everyone to sign a mutual agreement to end their contracts," he said.

"What did you tell him?"

"I told him he knows where he can put his mutual agreement."

"You didn't say that."

"I didn't," he chuckled, "perhaps I should have."

"How did he take it?"

"He began shouting at me. He thinks I have been spreading rumors around."

"You mean that the company is facing a hard time?"

"No, that has become the official version," he chuckled again. "Take my advice, don't sign that fucking thing. They want to get rid of us so that they will be finally able to sell the company. And if they are forced to fire us, they will have to pay each of us for the duration of the notice period. We shouldn't make it easy for them."

Later that day Katharina from Human Resources walked to my desk and placed a hand on my shoulder. "Hey, Tony. Alexander wants to talk to you."

I followed her to a meeting room. I liked that one. It had fish nets and seashells hanging from the ceiling as decorations and a ship's wheel had been nailed on a wall. The squared man was sitting there; he didn't even look at me as I entered and took a seat in front of him. Katharina sat next to him.

He wore a polo shirt with short sleeves and I thought there was something wrong with his arms. They couldn't possibly belong to that stout mass of squareness. He had tiny, flabby arms that came out of those sleeves and looked even more bizarre when they moved. As if they didn't belong to the body they were attached to and functioned under their own will. I was about to be interrogated by Finn the Human.

"I have reasons to believe you have been spreading around false rumors," he said.

I glanced at Katharina. "You mean about the company's financial situation?" I asked.

"The company is facing some hard times, that is true."

"So what are the other rumors?"

"You tell me."

"What do you want me to say?"

"The truth. Have you been spreading the rumor that we are attempting to sell the company?"

"Why would I do such a thing?"

"You are working against the company, perhaps?"

"Why would I work against the company that pays my salary?" I tried to pull the most outraged expression I could.

"Reprisal, maybe," he said as if he was taking a wild guess.

"Reprisal?" I said with a scandalized tone. "Everyone here has always acted nicely to me." For some reason that got Katharina smiling; the squared man didn't notice her. "I have no reason to hold any grudges."

"I'm pleased to hear that," he said with a smirk.

I shrugged.

"I just want to make sure that we are on the same page," he said.

"Sure."

"What about your manager, Santi?"

"What about him?"

"Is he spreading rumors?"

"Why are you worried about him?"

"I have been told about his misconduct."

"By who?" I asked.

"That is none of your concern," he said.

"Is it the same person who told you about me spreading rumors?"

He didn't reply to that answer. "You see, Antonio, since we are going through some hard times," he gently touched Katharina's arm, who promptly retreated from his grasp, "we are asking people to step back to ensure the survival of this company."

"I understand."

"I need you to sign this," he handed me a paper.

I read it.

"It reads that I will be released in one month," I said. "Well, according to my contract the company must give me a three months' notice period if you decide to fire me. One month is not enough to find another job. You know that better than me."

"It is for the survival of this company. Besides, if you meet us halfway, not only will we write a nice reference letter for you, but we will inform the Job Center right away for you to receive the unemployment allowance."

"I see."

"And there is more, you will have the opportunity to apply to one of the other companies of the Platypusnetic network. One of them is sending their recruiters to our office tomorrow for a first candidate screening. So?" He handed me a pen.

"I am sorry, man," I said. "I can't accept."

"Well, then, have a good day Antonio." He pointed at the door without looking at me.

The following day, the Platypusnetic recruiters came and camped out in one of our meeting rooms for the entire day. I didn't bother to find out what their company did, but Santi told me it was another business clone. Most of our colleagues went to have an interview with them. Santi, I, and a few others stayed at our desks, working on our tasks or pretending to do so. Well, at least I was pretending.

I was reading the news when Karim walked to my desk. "Hey Antonio," he leaned toward me with discretion, "these people came to interview you guys, why don't you go?"

I looked straight into his eyes. "Would you go if you were me?" I asked him.

He studied me as if he hadn't expected that question. "No," he said and walked away. Honesty, at last.

He, like the other executives, had been instructed by the squared man to persuade as many as he could to go to those interviews.

The following day, Leonard and the squared man informed Karim that they could no longer have him on the payroll and fired him.

*

I signed for two months of garden leave, which meant that I got paid for the following two months without having to do any work. That looked like a good deal to me. Santi signed it too, but in less than a week another company had offered him a job as their Marketing Director.

I kept sending my resume around and went to a few interviews but for the most part I took the time I had been given.

"How did it go?" Marina asked when I returned from one of the interviews.

"Awful," I said. "There were these two guys. One of them was this tall and skinny neat guy who kept staring at his bicep while he flexed it."

"While they interviewed you?"

"Yeah, I was talking and this guy kept flexing his bicep while the Gimli gave me the crazy stare."

"The Gimli?" She laughed.

"Every company is run by a Legolas and a Gimli. Legolas is the well-groomed one, he usually has that slicked back hairstyle and has a background in things like sales or marketing. The Gimli looks like a human accident and, being the nerd of the two, has experience in IT. He also lacks any form of emotional intelligence."

"What is it that this company does?" Marina asked.

"They produce food for people who are into fitness. They call it *super-food*."

"Why would you want to work there?"

"I've kept asking this same question to myself for years."

She gave me that understanding look. "Then do something else," she said.

"Like what?"

"I don't know, find something else if you've grown so weary of doing marketing."

"And start all over again? I'm twenty-nine, I can't go back to being an intern."

"What's wrong with that?"

"I can't. We can't. We have standards now. Okay, we still live in this place... oh, here they go again," I said as the neighbors upstairs were having another fight. The black woman went on with her usual *jaaaas* and *neeeins*.

"But we do have standards," I said, "what about our trips?"

Then it occurred to me that I was the one worried about trips and going out to restaurants. It doesn't happen every day, I thought, that people are more worried about the self-fulfillment of their partner than having enough money to go eat sushi every week. All along she had kept me from completely losing touch with reality. From being sucked into the mouth of the monster.

"You know what?" I said while holding her by the waist. "Let's just make good use of this time we have. Something will come along."

"I like the sound of that," she said.

We made very good use of that time and next thing I knew a company had offered me a job as their Marketing Director.

*

That's right. Their recruiter saw my LinkedIn profile and contacted me. After three interviews, the first with the same recruiter, the second with a guy who worked in marketing, and the third with one of the founders, they gave me the job. I had become good at interviews.

It was a small startup named YOLO Digital that employed twenty people at most. They had come up with a machine learning software for insurance plans. Their customers inserted their personal information such as age, gender, sexual orientation, occupation, income, pre-existing conditions, sports practiced, hobbies, smoking, drinking or drug habits, and the software would suggest the most fitting insurance plan for each of them. YOLO Digital would get a commission for each new customer they referred to the insurance companies through the software.

One of the founders was this rapper type. "What's up, bro? I am so humbled to have you on board." He wore a cap and a hockey jersey that must have been two sizes too big. He had the whole hip hop thing going on. He talked like one of those rappers, moved his hands like them, he was pulling some kind of hip hop show right in front of me. Marlon was his name.

"Me too," I said.

"Wanna know why I am so excited?"

"Please, tell me."

"I look at you right now and I see a hustler. In this company we only hire hustlers. I bet you're the kind of dude who gets his shit done. You don't fuck around."

"I try not to," I said.

"You see, this is like when Cleveland drafted LeBron. You are a top player in the industry. You got the SWAG!"

"What's that?"

"What?"

"That thing you said, the swag."

"Oh man, you kill me!" He clapped his hands and giggled. "Bro, it's time for you to learn some new terminology. You're from Italy, right?"

"Yeah."

"You know, I grew up in a tough neighborhood and hung out with some tough Italians. Those dudes got the SWAG."

The other founder kept a lower profile. He was into Hawaiian shirts. His name was Tilo, and I had to report to him every Monday in a meeting.

"We just got two million in funding. This is big shit, and we now need to show our investors that our AI tool is working like a charm. Let's advertise the shit out of it. Make everyone know about us," Tilo said during our first weekly meeting.

"Right on," I said. "What we need is a solid lead generation strategy."

"Absolutely," he said. "You bring us the leads and our girls will take care of the rest."

"I will start right away. What has been done so far?" I asked.

"Marketing-wise?"

"Yeah, marketing-wise."

"We attended fairs and other B2B and B2C events. We also started a partnership with a magazine."

"What magazine?"

"*B2Coolio*," he said.

"Sounds interesting. What is it about?"

"Hip hop for the most part, but they also have a business column. They invited us to their annual party two months ago. There were DJs and models. Cool shit." He said *cool* with a strong German accent.

"That is impressive," I said. "What about online marketing?"

"We have the Marlon's Tribune going out every week. You should have a look at it."

"What's that?"

"Every week we shoot a video of Marlon talking about cool stuff. It's the real shit. This week's video is about life in Berlin."

"What about Facebook ads? This could be a good start for now," I suggested.

"The guys have given it some tries, but it didn't really work. Boris will give you more information."

I went to this guy, Boris. "What's up, Boris? Tilo told me you're the go-to-guy for Facebook ads."

"Hi," Boris said. He was a very skinny guy, with massive eye bags.

"Do you mind showing me what you have done so far?"

"Sure." I could barely hear him as he spoke. He lay his Club-Mate bottle on his desk and opened the Facebook ads dashboard. "These are the ads," he said, "and these are the stats."

I nodded, I had never dealt with Facebook ads before. On my resume they must have seen I was more into SEO than an all-rounder marketer, but for some reason that didn't matter to them.

"As you can see," he kept talking slowly and with his muffled voice, "our ad-score is very low. I had tried to tweak a few things, but with little success." He stared at me as if he was waiting for me to say something smart.

"It's either the picture you used or the target audience," I guessed. "I will come up with something after lunch."

He gave me another dull stare. "Okay," he whispered.

At 1 pm I quickly went out, smoked a cigarette, bought a turkey sandwich, and returned to the office. With the sandwich in my hand I began searching on the Internet for everything there was to know about Facebook ads. I googled *Facebook ads for dummies* and found two blogs that seemed reliable and explained the thing in a way that even I could understand. I read one or two articles on each blog and within an hour I was a certified Facebook ads expert.

Boris returned from lunch break and as he walked by my desk, I waved at him. "Hey Boris, check this out."

He took off his jacket and bent over my screen. "What have you done?" he asked.

"For one thing, I have taken off the picture of that smiley hipster guy with that floral shirt," I said.

He looked at me with those dead fish eyes. He had another bottle of Club-Mate in his hand and only at that moment did I notice the floral pattern on the shirt he was wearing.

"I just believe we should present ourselves in a more inclusive manner to our customers," I added.

He nodded.

"Then I had a look at the target audience," I said. "May I ask you why you selected hip hop as an interest for our audience?"

"It was Tilo's idea," he said, sipping the Club-Mate.

"I see. Well, I reactivated the ads. Let's wait for Facebook to approve it and hopefully we should get some leads soon."

"Cool," he said.

"Thanks for your help, Boris."

"Sure," he whispered.

I turned to my screen, imagining that he would walk to his desk but as I turned around, he still stood there. He was looking at my sandwich which was still almost untouched. "You want a bite?" I asked.

"No, thanks," he said. "What's in it?"

"Turkey and salad. And some white sauce I have never seen before. I still have a hard time comprehending this country's fixation for sandwich sauces."

"It's with meat," he hinted with his muffled voice.

"Yeah, you know. It's turkey."

"I don't eat meat."

"Then I will finish it myself," I took a bite.

He glared at the sandwich.

"So you are a vegetarian," I said. "Look, I must have a granola bar somewhere." I began rummaging in my bag.

"I'm a vegan," he said.

"Uh."

"I can't eat those either."

"Sorry man, they contain milk, right?"

"No, they don't."

"Chocolate then."

"No, chocolate is fine. They use dark chocolate." *This guy must spend half of his life examining ingredient labels*, I thought.

"What then?"

"It's the natural flavors," he revealed at last.

190

"WHAT? What's wrong with natural flavors?" I asked.

"They might contain egg-derived products."

How I wished someone would have told me before.

*

To my bewilderment those Facebook ads worked, and that got the people in that place thinking that I knew what I was doing.

"Tony, I have never seen so many leads coming in one day," said Sophie, one of the account managers.

"What did you do? What did you do?" cried Charlotte; she was another account manager.

Sophie and Charlotte were two physical representations of one singular entity. For some reason, they were only seen together. If one had to use the girl's room, the other one followed. If one began a diet, the other began it too. One was taller and the other shorter but they looked quite alike and did everything together. At times I even had the impression that they had the tendency to finish each other's sentences. There was something sinister about that.

"I asked all my buddies to register to our software. In return I will buy them a beer," I said.

They looked at me dazed.

"I am kidding," I said. "I have just published some Facebook ads, and it seems it's working."

They looked relieved. Then the door of our room sprang open and Marlon walked in. He had this habit of flinging the door open, not considering that someone could be standing right behind it when he did that.

He rushed to Charlotte. "Listen carefully, about all those leads we just got, I want you and everyone else," he was pointing at Sophie, Charlotte, and the other account managers, "to get in touch with them ASAP, call them if necessary. Be a pain in the ass. Don't give up of a fucking centimeter." He pulled some sort of Al Pacino motivational speech about opportunities, determination, humbleness – he had a thing for the word *humble* and all its derivatives – following one's dreams and so on.

When he was done with the speech he walked back with his head down, swaying his arms, and I imagined this must be the way all rappers walk. Then, when he had almost reached the door, he turned to me with a jerk. "Hey, Tony. Good job with those ads, bro. This is dope." He wore a pair of mask sunglasses that covered half of his face.

"That's what you hired me for," I smiled.

"Don't be modest, here we celebrate success. Shout out to you, bro!"

"Thank you, Marlon."

"I knew you were a hustler. This is why I wanted an Italian to fill this position, you guys don't work hard, you work smart. You have a flexible mindset." He began pulling another hip hop show. "You're a Guy Van Kerckhoven kind of guy. That's what we need. We need a fucking-Van Kerckhoven-guy in this fucking company. Peace bro, keep up the good work."

He walked off. I searched for the *fucking Guy Van Kerckhoven* on Google.

Guy Van Kerckhoven was a Belgium-born, American naturalized entrepreneur, best-selling author, speaker, and Internet personality. Best known for his work in digital marketing, he founded this-and-that media and so on. I checked YouTube for some of his famous motivational speeches. There was a video titled "Life advice from Guy Van Kerckhoven", and I thought why would anyone want to take life advice from someone who has spent most of his own life in front of a computer.

Guy kept repeating the word *hustle*, he defined himself as a hustler and went on giving advices on such things as *chase your dream, love what you do, work-hard-play-hard, be yourself, build smart, keep moving, live your passion, hustle once more, develop yourself as a brand, no excuses* and *know who you are*. And while he said those things, he was all worked up, and I thought perhaps I had chosen a video which he had recorded on a particularly bad day. But no, in every video the guy kept being pissed and banging his fist against the desk. And when he didn't speak in front of a computer but to real people, he kept punching into his palm and giving the crazy stare to the audience as if someone from the crowd had yelled, "hey Guy, wrap it up, we are only here for the free booze."

"Hey Michael," Michael was our graphic designer, "what about Guy Van Kerckhoven? Don't you think he takes himself a bit too seriously?" I asked.

"I guess," he said. "He is okay." He was not into the topic and kept working at his computer.

"Hey Boris, what do you think of Guy Van Kerckhoven?" I turned to him.

"Oh, Guy." All of a sudden he had revived. "He is cool. I love him," he cried and went on listing all his achievements and how he had inspired him and thousands of others. "He is the real deal. Everybody wants to be like him."

"Is he vegan too?"

"I can't tell for sure, but I read he doesn't eat during the day."

"What do you mean?"

"He has hired a trainer who taught him the benefits of eating at night. I'm thinking of giving it a try."

"You want to hire a trainer?"

"I don't have the money. I will try by myself."

Something is not right with the people of my generation. During the 60s and 70s everybody wanted to be Jimi Hendrix or Marlon Brando. In the 90s Kurt Cobain wrote "Smells Like Teen Spirit", then he shot himself and for some reason everyone began listening to Kanye West and following alternative dietary programs. We claim we want to change the world and are so concerned with what happens on the other side of the globe, but we look the other way when a woman is being assaulted or a homeless person is freezing to death before our very eyes.

*

On Wednesday they recorded the Marlon's Tribune and every Wednesday Marlon would come to the office wearing some ludicrous hat or golden chain. This time he had bought a pair of white sunglasses at a nearby Gucci store which covered almost his entire face. "When you hustle for eighty hours a week you need to find the time to spoil yourself," he said and sat on a stool, with his arms crossed, in front of a white screen.

Michael, our designer, behind the camera said "action" and Marlon began with his usual rapping pantomime about hustling, humbleness, and having a vision.

"Hey Mickey, do you have the time to edit some pictures for me?" I asked Michael a few days later. "I would like to use them for a Facebook ad."

"By when do you need them?"

"The sooner the better. Are you that busy?"

"I am still editing the last Marlon's Tribune video."

"How long do you think it will take?"

"At least one day more," Michael said.

"Uh, is it usually that long?"

"It normally takes me one full day, but this week I also had to work on the design of our new swag."

Here they go again with this swag thing, "what's that?"

"The merch we give away to our partners," Michael said. "Like t-shirts, necklaces, key chains, and baseball caps."

"We give those things to people working in insurance companies?" I asked.

"Yeah, sure," he said. "Also to our investors and other partners. Tilo is going to a tech fair in London; he wants to pitch to some investors. We are gonna need some swag."

He showed me the sketch of a t-shirt. It had the YOLO Digital logo printed in gold and a golden chain hanging from the last O. Below the logo a small quote in brackets read *Wake up, Hustle, Go To Sleep, Repeat.*

"Whose quote is this?" I asked him.

"It's Marlon's."

I took a look at the previous installments of Marlon's Tribune. Once recorded and edited, they got published on Facebook and on the other social media channels.

Given the amount of work they required, I expected to see loads of people writing a comment or at least showing their support by clicking on the 'Like' button. All the videos rarely scraped more than ten 'Likes' together, and most of those 'Likes' were given by the people who worked in our company. Charlotte, Sophie, Michael, Boris and the other account managers. And each video received usually one comment from the same guy: *Hey Marlon, you are great. Marlon, you're such an inspiration. These videos are the BOMB. Can't wait for the next one.*

I decided to address the topic with Tilo during our next meeting.

"Have you seen our new swag?" He said as I took a seat, "this shit is AWESOME."

"It's COOL," I said. "Listen, I need to talk to you about Michael."

"That Dutch fuck," he said affectionately.

"That Dutch fuck."

"What's wrong with him?"

"Nothing wrong, he is great. It's just that he is really busy."

"Aren't we all?"

"Sure," I said. "The thing is, he hardly finds the time to help me out with marketing."

Tilo looked confused. "He has been busy designing our SWAG but now he is back to work on Marlon's Tribune."

"We should talk about those videos too. Are you sure they are working?"

His face filled with dismay. "What do you mean?"

"I mean, it seems no one is really watching them. And considering the amount of work Michael has to carry out every week, perhaps we may reconsider some of our marketing strategy."

"You want to stop making Marlon's Tribune?" That sounded more like an accusation than a question.

"I didn't mean that," except I did, "but perhaps we might shift the focus more on other things. Like the Facebook ads. They are working quite well. Or content marketing. We should focus on content marketing if we want to maximize our return on investments in the long run."

"Sure, do that," he muttered as if he was doing me a favor, "but we need to focus on the COOL shit. Maybe we should give Marlon's Tribune more visibility. Spread the rumor. How can we do that?"

"We could publish it as sponsored content on Facebook, but I am not sure this is a good idea."

"Why not?" he exclaimed. "I think it's a COOL idea."

"We should promote content that would prompt people to try out our insurance software. Marlon hardly talks about insurance on those videos.

Besides, I think we ought to be a bit more inclusive."

"Why?" He looked as if he was close to panicking.

"We should try to reach a broader audience." I was trying to find the right words. "There are people out there who do not necessarily listen to hip hop and may get scared off by our communication style, yet they might be interested in trying our software."

"But our videos are COOL!" he moaned with that German accent. "WE MUST DO COOL SHIT. Listen to me, why don't you try to give Marlon more visibility? Use a Facebook ad. Spread our SWAG! I am sure it will work."

"All right," I said.

*

At the end of my first six months at YOLO Digital, the bank account balance read four thousand euros and the scale 72 kilos, 8 kilos lighter than when I had started working there. To many, those four thousand euros may look like peanuts. Well, not to someone who used to get to payday with less than ten euros left in his bank account.

I still had those circles under the eyes and people said I looked pale, stressed out. I had cut down the drinking, not the cigarettes though, and I was still smoking pot regularly at home with Marina.

Despite the eight kilos missing, the paleness, the eyebags, I looked fairly healthy. Or at least to a level that no one would flinch when they saw me walking by.

My senses were numbed, though, and so was my spirit. I felt I was close to losing it. It's different than when you're just an intern. Back when I was an intern, their form of control consisted of giving me manual tasks like the assembly of furniture. I knew my position in the company was temporary therefore my brain was still able to adjust to any possible scenario. Able to conceive a way out.

That evening we had Santi over for dinner. He brought some fancy bottle of Spanish red wine. "Try this and you will finally stop drinking that Italian piss of yours," he chuckled.

What I would do to hear that chuckle in the office I'm in now, I thought.

"I am here for the food you promised," he said.

We had prepared a dish from my region. Marina and I had decided to cut down on takeaways and begin cooking with more frequency. It had a soothing effect on me. It reminded of things one can do other than sitting for eight hours looking at a computer screen. We would usually build a joint beforehand and smoke it while cooking.

"Dude, she is gorgeous, smart, funny and she can even cook. What is she doing with you?" he said as we were done with the meal.

"And soon she will start her teaching career and support me after my early retirement."

He chuckled. "Are you going to support this lazy fuck?" Santi asked Marina.

"Sure, why not? He has been the main breadwinner. It's time to reverse some gender roles."

"At least one person in this room is going to have an impact on society," I said.

"True that," Santi agreed, "molding the future generations. And what are you going to do?"

"I will figure out something."

"Dude, you look tired. Did you smoke?"

"Only a few hits while preparing dinner," I said.

Santi chuckled again. "Any news from the insurance industry?"

"I don't know what you're talking about," I said bitterly.

"He is having a hard time dealing with all the hip hop going on in that place," Marina said.

"That must be hard on you," Santi chuckled.

"It's not only that," I said, "they want me to work on things that don't make any sense."

"Tony, why don't you come to my company? With you we would take our content marketing to the next level."

"I don't want to work for you," I said.

"You have always said you loved working for him and he is the best boss you have ever had," Marina said.

"He said that?" Santi cried.

"I don't want to spoil our friendship," I said.

"What makes you think you will spoil our friendship? I am not your friend to begin with," he laughed. The wine was already making him happy. Luckily, I had bought two more bottles for that evening.

"No, seriously," he went on, "you send me your resume, have a chat with our Managing Director, which will be only a formality, and you're in."

"Why don't you give it a try?" Marina asked. "It can't be worse than where you are now."

"Thanks man. As Marina said, I enjoyed working with you. But I want this job to be the last of its kind. I am sick of interviews, company events, cover letters. I am sick of pretending to give a shit. I would only be a pain in the ass for you."

"Think about it," he said. "Do you still have some of that weed?"

Marina and I sat on the couch and Santi began flipping through my vinyl collection. "You have quite a collection here!"

"He spent two hundred euros on vinyl last week," Marina said.

"I have to put the money I earn somewhere," I said.

"This is the one you always talked about." He played *Trout Mask Replica* by Captain Beefheart and His Magic Band.

He sat with us and we began passing the joint around.

"What about you?" Marina asked Santi. "Are you happy in your new job?"

"Of course he is," I said. "Give him a Google spreadsheet and a line graph and you make him happy. Look at his face."

He chuckled. "I am," he said, "lots of work to do but I can't complain."

"Are you still dating that lady from your team?" I asked him.

"On and off," he said. "I am trying to end it, you know, not to spread the rumor."

"Sleazy fuck," I said.

He chuckled. "What's happening upstairs?" Santi asked as our neighbors from upstairs started another fight.

"They are late. I was worrying," I said.

"They fight almost every day," Marina told him.

"Are they a couple?"

"It's this guy living with two women."

"And they fight all the time?" Santi laughed.

"The guy with one of the women. The other woman gets mixed up."

"They must have some kind of swing in there," I said.

Santi chuckled again.

"When they are not fighting we hear this squeaky noise," I said. "They must be doing nasty stuff in there.

"Does anyone ever complain?" Santi asked.

"People see it as part of the Wedding folklore."

Some time past eleven Santi left. "Think about my proposal," he mumbled. He was high and staggered as he walked to the door. He was quite a spectacle when he was high or drunk. "It would be great working together again. We would do great things."

"I will think about it," I said, only to please him.

Marina and I went back to the couch and rolled another joint.

"He is such a nice guy," Marina pointed out.

"He is," I said.

"What does his company do?"

"No idea."

"When you were in the bathroom he told me how he loved working with you. He said you were the best in his team."

"He said that?"

"I was surprised to be honest. I mean, you never talk about work."

"He is a great guy. I guess that was the reason I tried not to fuck up."

"So you made up your mind?"

"I think so. I will keep going until the expiration of my one year contract. In the meantime we will have saved enough to live off for a while and come up with something else."

"Tony."

"Yes?"

"I'm so proud of you," she said.

I looked her in the eyes. Those green, understanding eyes. They were still human, unspoiled. Perhaps they would change too one day.

"We could travel for a while before you start working at the school," I said.

"You still think of that place we visited in Southern Spain."

"I do."

The biggest burden many people suffer is not the lack of money, but rather the lack of time. Time to be able to come up with an escape plan. We are so drowned in our daily routine that our brains refuse to conceive there is another way. I just needed to endure another six months.

"Wanna watch something?" I proposed.

"Should we continue *Better Call Saul?*"

"We won't be able to stop after one episode. I'd like to get some sleep. How about *The Long Goodbye*?"

"That's a full length movie."

"Definitely worth the sleep deprivation," I said.

"It's okay with me," Marina said.

"I'll make some tea," I said and stood up.

I walked to the kitchen and, as I switched the light on, everything around me began to spin madly. In a fraction of a second my strength abandoned me, as if my mind was flying out of my body. Then everything became hazy.

I woke up to the squeaking noise of the small wheels of a stretcher somebody had placed me on. Blinding flashes coming in quick succession prevented me from realizing where I was. Two men were pushing the stretcher along a narrow corridor. They both wore face masks. I could only discern their silhouettes. They didn't look like nurses, nor doctors for all I knew. There was a stench in that place that prevented me from breathing normally. I began to gasp and in an attempt to rise on my elbows, I realized they had strapped me onto the stretcher. I couldn't move a centimeter. My entire body felt numb. Only my eyes were spared from that stillness.

I opened my mouth, trying to ask for an explanation. Not a sound came out and I began gasping more heavily.

They kept pushing the stretcher with me on it, until we reached a heavy metallic gate. One of the men pushed a button. The gate opened and they pushed me inside.

I looked around and couldn't believe my eyes. What kind of building could contain a place like that? Its expanse was maddening to comprehend. It had a circular shape, hollow at the center, like a humongous sinkhole surrounded by an endless series of glass tanks supported by metallic skeletons.

We got closer to those tanks and I saw they contained a formaldehyde-resembling liquid. Some of them were empty, except for the liquid, while others contained something that I was unable to identify at first.

Human bodies or what was left of them floated inside those tanks. They kept pushing the stretcher along that endless display of decaying bodies, which began to rattle as it slid on the metallic platform. I looked at them all as we passed by, one after the other; there was no way I could look away.

I don't know for how long they kept pushing that stretcher with me on it, but I must have seen hundreds of those rotting bodies. And that must have been only an insignificant part of the whole amount.

Then they stopped pushing and left me strapped on the stretcher. I still couldn't feel my body and couldn't speak.

I looked at some bodies floating inside those tanks only a few meters away, only to realize that they were still alive. Their skin had almost completely peeled off, revealing the purplish arteries and their muscular tissue. Part of their limbs had begun to dissolve into the formaldehyde-like liquid, as if they were being eaten by microscopic organisms, but their vigilant eyes were rolling madly as if they were screaming at me. A giant tube spurted out the top of each tank, descending into the sinkhole.

The two men returned and began pushing me again, this time only a dozen meters ahead, before walking away.

I looked at the bodies floating in front of me and recognized Marcus, my boss at The Dancing Avocado. Next to him was Lukas, then

I saw Leonard and the squared man. I saw Karim, then Benjamin and Kaspar from Go-Go Fashion.

Little of their original appearance was left. They were all there, gazing at me with those staring eyes that lacked eyelids and any form of emotion.

After a while, the two men returned again and pushed me along another display of decay. The degradation of the bodies seemed to diminish as we walked past them.

They stopped again. This time the decay of the bodies was still at its initial stage. They were practically intact as they floated inside the tanks. I recognized them too. My former colleagues at The Dancing Avocado were among them. Hector, Quique, Adriana, and Juan looked dully at me, motionless. I saw Marlon and Tilo. Santi was right in front of me. The tank next to his was empty.

The two men with the face masks returned and began to unstrap me from the stretcher. Another stood on a ladder, removing a metallic cover from the top of the empty tank.

As they carried me up the ladder, I still couldn't move nor speak. Then I heard that unearthly, shrill sound coming from the depths of that sinkhole. It was impossible to describe. Like a maddening cacophony of slithering gurgles.

A cold, artificial light reflected on the opposite rim, outlining an enormous mass of unraveling appendages scraping their way up the sinkhole.

They tossed my motionless body inside the tank and shut the metallic cover over me. The formaldehyde-like liquid swallowed me in an instant. I struggled to keep my eyes open. Then everything became hazy again.

When I opened my eyes, she was there, gently caressing my face with her cold fingers. She looked beautiful. Beautiful and terrified.

"What's happened?" I whispered.

"You fainted," Marina said trembling. "You scared me to death. Right after you walked to the kitchen, I heard a thud and rushed in here. I found you lying flat, unconscious."

"How long was I unconscious?" I asked her.

"About half a minute, then you smiled and began groaning, as if you were dreaming."

She was still holding my face.

"How do you feel?" She asked, rubbing her thumb on my forehead.

"I'm fine, actually. A bit dizzy perhaps." I managed to rise on my elbows. "What else did I do?"

"Well," she hesitated, "you let out a big fart. Fuck! I have never been so scared," she cried, still trembling.

"Jesus Christ, I'm sorry," I said.

Once a year in Berlin there is a day you wake up and you begin to think that you are in a different place. That dazzling white cape that for months cloaks the sky, preventing the sun's rays from descending, disappears. Even the people seem to give up the idiosyncratic *Schnauze*. It's not gone, it's still there, but they are too busy sunbathing in the park to scold you for standing in their way or for just being alive. And for a few months of the year you're tricked into thinking that you actually live in some idyllic place, surrounded by decent people.

It was a tepid day in May. The alarm rang at 8 am, like every working day, and as I looked outside, the whole place was illuminated. Like every morning, I had muesli and milk for breakfast, showered, dressed, and kissed Marina before leaving for work.

"How about I pick you up after work?" she asked.

"Sounds good," I said before heading to the U-Bahn station.

I got there earlier than usual and I could have started at 9 am instead of the usual 9.30 am and left earlier in the evening. Instead, I took my time and strolled on the sunlit sidewalk, contemplating the people who rushed to their jobs. Some wore formal clothes and carried leather briefcases, others were more casual, but they all looked alike except for the clothes they wore. A tall, well-dressed girl walked in the opposite direction. She kept her head down as she strode on those wedge heels. She was very pale and I imagined she was a model headed to one of the many modeling studios in that neighborhood.

That was a clean and neat neighborhood, with historical buildings that were spared during the WWII bombings. It was different from the neighborhoods I was used to going to work in, certainly miles away from where I lived despite being only a few metro stops away. I knew I didn't belong there and I thought of the Kreuzberg office during my time at The Dancing Avocado. By the way, months earlier Lukas and Marcus had sold The Dancing Avocado to a competitor and parted ways, while my former colleagues had to find another job.

The same source also told me that Marcus had broken up with Viktoria, the opulent woman with the lap dog. It happened only one week after her dog had died. The poor thing. Anyway, as a revenge, Viktoria thought it was a good idea to dig up the carcass of the poor beast and let Marcus find it in the basket of his bike before going to work in the morning. These are the kind of stories one wants to hear.

The shops, cafés, and kebab kiosks were opening as I walked past. In front of a supermarket was this man in a wheelchair. I had seen him many times and often I would hand him one or two euros. He was not too much older than me. He had a thick head of blond hair and big, deep green eyes that seemed able to peer right into my soul each time I got close to him. He was a beautiful man but he had no arms and no legs. He had nothing, but his eyes were more alive and deeper than those of the people I saw on that sidewalk with their coffee mugs and smartphones. I rummaged in my wallet only to find coins of two or five cents. I found a twenty euro bill and stuffed it into a paper cup that someone had placed on the armrest of his wheelchair. I would have spent it on some record, anyway. I felt in a good mood that morning, for some reason.

"Thanks," he said in English with a clever smile. He must have become aware of my poor German skills during our previous encounters.

I greeted him and walked to the office where my mood quickly worsened.

It was one of those lazy, hot days at work when all you want to do is sink into your chair and not talk to anyone. For the last few weeks I had been hellbent on making those Facebook ads cool, as Tilo had requested, with poor results and people had stopped registering to our platform.

Everyone in the company began to panic as the volume of commission we got from the insurance companies began to shrink.

Whenever I had the chance, I went to the backyard to smoke a cigarette, making sure that Sophie and Charlotte were not there. Whenever I had got close to them in the previous weeks, they threw on me all their concern for the lack of leads. Well, I'm quite certain they didn't give a shit about the leads. They were only true to their game role. Like the rest of us, after all.

"WHY ARE WE GETTING SO FEW LEADS?" they stood in front of me, one next to the other, forming a perfect line and smoking cigarettes from the same brand.

"Something is not working with the Facebook ads," I explained.

"BUT THEY WERE WORKING BEFORE."

"I have made some changes."

"WHY?"

"Tilo asked me to."

"SO WHAT'S WRONG NOW?"

"Why don't you ask him?"

"WHAT?"

"I'm trying to figure it out," I said.

So, this time I smoked my cigarettes in peace, then went back to my desk and sank again into the chair. Marlon sprang the door open and walked past my desk without acknowledging my presence. He had stopped talking to me since, a couple of weeks earlier, I had told him I didn't listen to hip hop.

"What is your favorite hip hop artist?" he had asked me back then.

"I don't listen to hip hop." I confessed at last.

He gave me a disbelieved look and walked away. I thought I had hurt him somehow.

Marlon walked to Charlotte's desk. "Why so serious? SMILE," he demanded. "Pretty girls should smile." Then he asked her to follow him to his office, where he began yelling at her. When she returned, she was crying and Sophie rushed to console her. It was not uncommon to see Charlotte crying because of Marlon yelling at her.

When quiet descended again, I got back to work on those Facebook ads. For some delusional reason, I thought I was close to finding a solution, when I began hearing springy noises and sneers. I turned around and I saw Boris and Michael holding foam dart guns and shooting each other using their respective computer screens as shields.

"Do you want a gun, Tony?" Boris asked.

"Thanks, I have stuff to do," I said and turned again to my screen. Michael handed two more toy guns to Sophie and Charlotte as they too joined the fray. I put my headphones on and increased the volume. Marc Bolan's guitar was doing serious harm to my eardrums, when I felt one of those foam darts hitting the back of my neck.

I turned and saw Boris staring at me with an idiotic grin.

"Buddy, cut it. I AM TRYING TO MAKE THE SWAG HERE," I begged him and returned to my task.

The shooting went on, interrupted only by Marlon's frequent

incursions. Each time he would burst the door open more noisily than the previous time, and I thought he was doing it purposely to drive me mad.

"You look like a bunch of retards," he would tell the shooters and giggle as he entered our room.

I kept increasing the music volume but the bursts of the door, Marlon's giggles, the springy noise of the foam darts being shot, and the sneers were all over me.

Then another foam dart landed on the top of my head.

"DUDE, I TOLD YOU I AM TRYING TO GET SHIT DONE HERE," I growled at Boris.

"You are so passive aggressive, Tony," Boris groaned.

It was 5 pm, time for my weekly meeting with Tilo.

When I entered his room, I flinched. Tilo was almost unrecognizable as the left side of his face had swollen, forming a purplish lump below his eye. Tilo was two years younger than me, but was partially bald and had a sagging belly. "I am too busy hustling to eat," he would proudly claim when lunch time struck. But, according to Michael, when he got out from work at 9 pm he would stuff that sagging belly with a king size portion of nachos topped with melted cheese and jalapeños while playing *FIFA 17* on his couch.

"Tony, I have the investors on my back. We barely get any leads." Tilo sweated and trembled; he had just returned from a meeting with the investors.

I tried not to stare at that purplish lump. "Let's put the old ads back," I promptly suggested, "just give me the okay and I will reactivate them right away."

"I have told you we must stick to the cool stuff," he growled.

"I did everything you said. I even tried to give more visibility to Marlon's videos. It's just a waste of budget. Let me reactivate the old ads. In the meantime we can think of something."

"YOU WANT TO STOP MAKING MARLON'S TRIBUNE?"

"Only for a few weeks. Boris and Michael will have more time to help me with the ads and content marketing. When the leads are back we can give the Tribune another try."

Tilo was now trembling, sweat descended his forehead, and I got the impression the lump was increasing in size. His face looked like that of a roughed-up pugilist. *Look at what the startup dream has done to this man*, I thought.

"NO," he roared. "WE CAN'T GIVE UP THE TRIBUNE. WE MUST DO COOL SHIT."

"I am resigning, Tilo," I said at last. I didn't intend to quit. Not yet anyway. It just came out.

Tilo didn't look surprised and I got the impression that he had given some thought to firing me before. It was a matter of weeks, perhaps days, before that actually happened, and I just came first.

I felt good. I hadn't felt that good in months.

We came to an agreement to let me go with immediate effect and in exchange I committed to not claim the money for the vacation days I had not yet taken. I signed all the papers and shook hands with Tilo. Somehow he looked relieved too.

When I left, Marina was waiting outside. She looked beautiful as she stood on the sidewalk, smoking a cigarette and smiling at me.

I smiled back at her like I hadn't done in months, clung to her, and kissed her.

We then walked down the sunlit sidewalk.

"You know what?" I said to her.

"Tell me."

"Perhaps I can finally learn German."

"Yeah, right…"

*

Some days later I received a message from Hector

¿qué tal cabron? I will be in town tomorrow for the big fiesta. I have already told the others. Are you in? Do not let me down.

That year, for the first time, I had spared myself the hassle of attending the May Day in Kreuzberg.

It's the same story every year. You wake up and embark on a draining text message exchange with your pals to agree on a meeting place and a time that suits everyone. You take the metro which runs at irregular intervals due to the crowd, get out of the packed train still with the smell in your nostrils of the sweaty armpits of a guy with a top knot who decided to wear a tank top on that particular day. White guys and tank tops. Jesus Christ. When you're out of the metro, you find yourself swept away by a tide of fellow millennials dancing to blaring techno music. Then you try to make your way through the crowd to meet your friends who are waiting for you on the other end of the street. It takes you forty five minutes to fight your way out of those sixty meters of dancing hipsters and gutter punks, and when you have finally made it, your friends are not there. Only then you grab your phone from your pocket and find a message from your friend that reads *Sorry, man. I got too loaded yesterday. Still at home, I am going to be a little late.*

Since going back is not an option, alone and resigned, you try to make the best out of the situation. You get something to drink as fast as you can and wander around, then eventually you bump into some former colleague you haven't seen in a while. You begin drinking and smoking and three or four hours are gone. Then your friends arrive. "Where the fuck have you been?" They cry, "We have been looking for you for hours."

You carry on drinking and smoking with your friends, and in the meantime some angry extreme left-wing guy with a hoodie thinks it is a good idea to throw a brick against a shop window because, what the hell, that too is freedom of expression. That gives the right excuse to some even angrier fascist cop with the face of Putin tattooed on his butt cheek to begin beating the shit out of everyone or everything within reach that breathes. And some nostalgic twisted mind would say that too is freedom of expression.

I get it's all about freedom of expression, but I might as well celebrate that by smoking a joint on my couch while listening to Frank Zappa. Or, well, Captain Beefheart. They were buddies, after all.

Anyway, even if it wasn't for the damned May Day, Hector pulled me in for the Carnival of Culture.

I went with Santi. We found Hector and Adriana drinking beer outside a bar on Bergmannstrasse.

"*Hermano*," Hector stood up and hugged me. He looked neater since the last time we met. There was little left of the Southern Spanish boy I remembered. He had begun working out and now sported that slicked back hairstyle, shorter on the back and on the sides. His beard was perfectly trimmed too, but I was glad to realize that the transformation hadn't altered his jovial manners.

"He is still alive," Adriana cried. "Where the fuck have you been?"

"Where is Marina?" they asked.

"Meeting some friends. She is joining us later."

Quique, Juan, and other people came too.

"*Cabrones*," Quique yelled as they approached.

"How I missed those beautiful faces," Hector said while I introduced Santi to them.

"Let's get some beer and go check the parade," Quique proposed.

Each of us got a beer and we slowly made it to the parade. The Costa Rica float came first, then it was the turn of Sierra Leone and Lebanon. We stood there for a while, drinking and chatting, then we walked to a park and sat there in a circle.

They had set up a small stage on which a three piece band was performing a gig. The woman who was the lead singer started to chant an eerie litany accompanied by the warlike drum percussion of another band member, while the third sketched a guitar riff which expanded as the song progressed.

"Are you really going for it?" Hector asked me as we sat quietly sipping our beer and watching the gig.

"Sure, why not? I guess it's too late to ask for my job back, anyway."

"But do you have a plan?"

"Not really. Marina and I are thinking of traveling for a while. I have saved enough to live off for the next few months. After that I could take unemployment money for a while. It's time for the *Bundesrepublik* to repay me for many years of hard work."

"All I am saying, it really takes guts," Hector said.

"You call it guts, I call it common sense," I said.

For some reason that made Hector laugh.

The percussion became louder and louder, like the lumbering steps of some gigantic being set to run over the celebrations with all the floats, the beverage kiosks, and the people in them. There was something ominous and at the same time reassuring about that chant. At times it made my teeth rattle, at others all I wanted was to let that sound embrace me and cradle me to a deep sleep.

"I admire you for it. If things weren't going this well at work, I would do the same," Hector said. "Have I told you I have been promoted to Regional Head of Sales? They gave me these three minions who do everything I say. But man, how I miss this dirty town."

"I'm happy for you," I said. "You deserve it."

"London is cold as fuck. I mean, the people are cold. It's not easy to make friends. But you know what? If I keep working there, in three years I would make enough to buy me an apartment."

"You want to settle down there?"

"Fuck no, I will buy something back home."

"That sounds like a reasonable plan," I said.

The gig was over and so was the parade. The sun had begun its descent into the late spring night, and the celebrations were slowly blowing over.

Hector, Santi, Quique, and I walked to a nearby Spätkauf to buy more beer and returned to the park where we kept drinking and chatting until past midnight.

Then I got a message from Marina, *I'll be there in fifteen minutes. Can you meet me at the U-Bahn station?*

"I'm going to get Marina," I told the guys. "I'll be back in ten minutes. Will I find you here?"

"Nothing on earth will make me move my fat Spanish ass from here," Quique said as he lay on the grass.

"I quote him," said Santi who lay right next to him. The two were talking with Adriana and Juan about the house market in Berlin, as Juan was considering starting a mortgage with his girlfriend. Hector sat a few meters away with the others.

"Shall we move somewhere else when you return?" Hector proposed.

"Yes!" Quique cried. "Let's go to the Pie, like in the good old times."

Everyone agreed. The Pie was a small bar near The Dancing Avocado office and the place where we would often conclude the day back then.

"Tony," Juan called me and handed me what was left of a joint, "for the way, *hermano*."

I took it and began walking down the scarcely illuminated pathway that crossed the park. Small groups of party goers were scattered around the park and the street.

It was nice to see the guys again. It was as if the last couple of years hadn't happened.

The night was young and Berlin was just waking up. It's all about finding your own place, after all.

*

"Forget about all that crap," Bernhard said as he sat on a stool at the counter next to mine, "life has to be lived. We are animals for Christ's sake. You can't sit on a chair for eight hours a day pretending everything is fine."

"Could you please refill?" I asked the bartender across the counter. She gave me a puzzled look then turned to Bernhard.

"I'll have what he has," he said to the bartender.

"Gotta light?" I asked Bernhard.

"Sure, buddy," he lit my cigarette, "all I am saying, we are still young. We ought to travel, meet people, broaden our horizons, for Christ's sake. Don't let anyone drag you down. Let's go out and suck out all the marrow of life. You and me," he yawped.

"It's raining," I said as the rain beat loudly on the trembling wooden door of the bar. Thunder could be heard in the distance.

"Tony, *hermano*." Someone grabbed my shoulder. It was Juan. "Wanna smoke with us?"

I turned and saw a tall figure sitting at a small table in a dark corner of the bar. A candle stood in the middle of the table, its flame powerful and firm. I recognized Liam.

"What's up mate? Fancy a toke?" Liam asked.

I followed Juan and we sat at the table with Liam. They were talking about football and sharing a joint.

"Man, Le Tissier was an incredible finisher," Juan cried.

"Lazy fuck," Liam said.

"Yeah, but when you have his intelligence on the ball you don't need to run a lot," Juan insisted.

"That is true," Liam said and handed the joint back to Juan. "What about Gazza?"

By then the rain was beating viciously against the door.

"Fucking genius."

"HE WAS SICK, SICK, SICK."

"What are you sissies talking about?" Joe approached our table. I hadn't seen Joe since the day he left The Dancing Avocado.

"Do you think Robert Prosinečki was the better playmaker over Le Tissier?" Juan asked Joe.

"Both only good for medium-flight sides. I am getting the fuck outta here," Joe said and headed to the door.

"Dude, wait, it's pouring!" I shouted and went after him. But Joe had already disappeared into the thick rain. The street, the other buildings, cars, bikes – everything had disappeared. *We found ourselves stranded on a rock at the mercy of the stormy sea.*

I returned inside.

The draft of the door being shut made the candle flame writhe and spin, like in some mad dance, before returning still.

Juan and Liam kept smoking and talking about football.

I walked back to the counter and noticed three women sitting at another table. Each of them had a beer. They were not talking, only staring at their glasses. As I moved a few steps closer, I recognized Lucia, Monica, and Alessandra, my former Italian colleagues. Only then Lucia lifted her head and saw me. She was expressionless and looked at me as if she was trying to make sense of what she was seeing.

Then someone bumped my back. "Dude, are these chicks with you?" he said, only to retreat after getting close enough to the table.

"What a fetid shithole is this place," Karim said. I saw Marlon and the squared man standing in the shadows behind him. "Dude, check this." Karim raised his wrist, revealing a silver watch. "Ten grand. Can you believe it?"

Then lightning struck right outside the bar. The entire place began to shake madly. The heavy rain relentlessly beat on the door which was on the verge of being shattered. The few electric lights tilted and flickered, leaving the entire place dark for a few seconds. It was as if the world was ending right at that moment.

"Tony, where is your glass, *cabron*?" I heard Quique shouting.

He stood with Adriana at the other end of the counter.

"You promised to have one with us," Adriana said.

"Let's have Jäger shots. WAIT, let's have whisky," Quique said.

"Why don't we just have both?" Adriana proposed.

"YES, let's have both. Tony, isn't she just a magnificent woman?" Quique asked.

"She is," I said.

"I miss having you as a colleague, Tony." Adriana clung to my arm and plunged her face into my waist. I couldn't see her face as it was hidden by her disheveled, dark blond hair and she felt exceptionally light as she leaned on me. "You are a good person," she whispered.

Thunder kept shaking the ground and the rain kept falling tirelessly. The lights flickered again, as if the ceiling was about to collapse on us anytime.

Quique handed me and Adriana shot glasses. "To the good old times," he toasted.

We drank the Jäger shots, then Quique passed the whisky shots. "To the future," he toasted again and we gulped the whisky as a thunder made the glass of the window rattle.

"I am going to the bathroom," I said.

"Do not disappear again," Adriana said.

As I walked to the men's room, I found Anna in the narrow hallway that led to the bathrooms. She smiled and said something I couldn't hear due to the loud music. The radio was now playing "Nightclubbing".

I got closer to her as she spoke in my ear. "Are you having a good time?" she asked and flattened herself against the wall.

"I am," I said in her ear while her perfume bit my nostrils. "Sure, I am."

She gave me a doubtful look. "Wanna smoke with me?"

I took two cigarettes out of the pack, handed her one and lit it as she placed it between her lips.

"Thanks," she said and gently stroked my face with both hands as I noticed someone walking out of the men's room. The figure scurried in our direction and I recognized Marcus and his frantic eyes. He slowed his pace and glared at me as he moved past. His eyes were full of hate but they also showed fear, the fear of just another frightened soul running toward the storm and disappearing into it.

Then thunder made the place shake viciously and all the lights went off. In that darkness only the candles on the tables glowed.

When the lights returned, Anna was gone.

I walked to the men's room and found Hector and Santi peeing at the urinals, leaving free the one in the middle, which I took.

"What are you going to do now?" Hector asked me.

"I will just take it easy and see what comes next," I said.

"Tony, you know there will always be a place for you in my team," Quique said.

"Thanks, man," I said.

"What great things we would do together again," he added.

"You mean getting drunk in the workplace?" Hector asked.

Santi chuckled. "That as well. But this guy knows a great deal about content marketing."

"Are you so tired of doing SEO?" Hector asked me.

"I guess I need to figure out what I want to do," I said.

"I admire you for that, Tony," Hector said.

They both zipped their pants and walked away. "Let's get something to drink, Tony."

"I'll catch you in a minute," I said.

I zipped my pants, washed my hands, and took a look at the mirror. The rain and the thunder could be heard from the men's room. I washed my face; it looked surprisingly fresh on that nightmarish evening, despite the booze and the joint. I felt good, I had never felt that good.

As I walked out of the men's room, an icy blast of air passed through my body. The hallway was entirely dark as the electric lights had now stopped working for good. I could feel my bones freezing. The music was still on but I couldn't hear anyone.

I heard the rain beating on the wooden floor of the bar, the thunder roaring, and the wind making its way in. The door was flapping madly and the window shattered into pieces, while my shoes were now soaked by the water that flooded the place.

There was no one left in the bar.

*

The day after I was awoken by Marina leaping out of bed and walking to the bathroom. She would usually get out of bed before me on weekends.

I checked the phone. Four minutes to 11 am. It was a hell of a sunny day outside. I never liked Sundays. I began reading the news on my phone.

The conflict in Libya continued; the Russiagate investigations had unveiled alleged Russian interference in the 2016 US elections; a seventeen-year-old had poured gasoline over his sweetheart and watched her burn alive in an abandoned farmhouse in the Italian countryside; a child of a few months old born to vegan parents had died of malnutrition.

I placed the phone on the night stand and closed my eyes.

At least one can sleep on Sunday. Perhaps Marina and I can have breakfast at the bar across the street. They have those croissants filled with crème patissière that you hardly find elsewhere in town. I could have one of those with a coffee. Then we could take a walk around Wedding. There is always something worth-seeing in our neighborhood. After that we return home, make a joint and watch some TV show until it gets darker again. We could order cheeseburgers for dinner, or maybe Chinese. I'll ask Marina what she thinks. That would give some meaning to that Sunday.

Then I was in that place where you are not asleep but not awake either. I liked that. I let the Sunday morning noises of Wedding lull me.

Then a scream came from the bathroom. "SHIT."

I opened my eyes and another scream came. "OH SSSHIT. SHIT! SHIT!"

Then I heard Marina open the bathroom door and slowly walk to the bedroom.

"What's going on?" I rose on my elbows as she leaned against the edge of the door. Her eyes were moist. She held something in one hand and covered her mouth with the other.

"Are you alright?"

She slowly moved the thing she held in my direction.

"It's positive," she said.

Police sirens darted down the street. The neighbors upstairs were having a fight. A Turkish man was screaming at his wife, or at his daughter. Hard to tell.

Life in Wedding went on undisturbed.

*

One week later… more or less.

Dear Hiring Manager,

I am reaching out in response to the opening for the position of SEO Manager as listed on your website.

With regard to the competencies you are looking for to fill the position, I can offer you six years of experience as an in-house marketer for top-notch Berlin's digital firms with particular emphasis on SEO, Content Marketing and Social Media.

My strong analytical and creative approach to the craft of campaign conceptualization for companies like Dumboo and YOLO Digital has resulted in a track record of successful communication initiatives featured in top tier European media outlets, all of which should make me an ideal fit for this opening.

I'm looking for a role that challenges me, allows me to expand my existing skills, and to make a tangible contribution to the company's success.

I have attached my resume for your review and would welcome the chance to speak with you at your earliest convenience.

Best regards,
Antonio La Matina

First published in 2022

ragingsloths.tumblr.com